Now I Lei Me Down To Sleep

A Briar Malone Mystery

Casey Ward, Author

Now I Lei Me Down To Sleep

A Briar Malone Mystery

Casey Ward, Author

Cover Designed by Voodoo Graphics.

Casey Ward

A Briar Malone Mystery Thriller

Now I Lei Me Down To Sleep

Chapter 1

The muted engine sound from inside the airplane cabin was almost hypnotic, as Briar eased her seat back for a more comfortable position. The Flight Attendant had cleared the meal trays, and was now serving coffee and liqueurs. Briar declined the offer with a smile and a wave of her hand, as she turned back to the window. It was a clear evening as the United Boeing 757 sliced through the night air. The sky was bright with a million stars, while thousands of lights outlined Chicago as they flew thirty-five thousand feet above it. Briar was exhausted and just wanted to sleep for the next four hours, until they landed at LAX. Her decision to leave New York and her legal investigator job (working for Spencer &

Davis Law firm) all happened so fast, that she hadn't had time to think too deeply about what she was doing. She just knew it was the right decision, and once she'd settled into her new apartment and gotten herself situated, everything would be fine. That was the way it always happened for her…one door closed and another opened. Not always for the better, but always better than the room she had just left. There were many rooms that she would love to peek back into, just to see how things turned out, but then…there were others she dared not ever open again. Regardless of how far Briar had come in her twenty-nine years and how much she had accomplished, she couldn't overcome her feeling of inadequacy. She still found ways to sabotage any good thing that happened to her. As the cabin lights dimmed and Briar began to doze, she wondered if she would ever be able to put her ugly past behind her.

Briar—The early years…

In April of 1992, a few days before Briar's sixth birthday, she was left by her maternal

Grandmother, in the foyer of a local orphanage called "The Home for Little Wanderers." Since birth, she had lived in St. Joseph, Missouri with her biological mother, Donna Sandusky—a raging crack cocaine addict, who cared only about where her next fix was coming from. She got pregnant with Briar while in a court-mandated rehab seven years prior. After the loser that knocked her up was released from rehab, he went back to live with his wife and family. Nine months later, Briar was born…the unwanted result of that month long rehab hook-up.

Donna was from a poor local Polish family, which had neither the means nor the desire to take on another child to rear. Although she was urged to give the fiery red-haired baby up for adoption, she opted instead to drag Briar from crack house to flop house, mainly because it meant she could draw a steady welfare check, receive food stamps, and qualify for other government benefits. She stripped at various dive clubs around town, when she wasn't too drunk or stoned to hang onto the pole. Men were a means for drugs, and she used whatever she had to keep that flow coming. She frequently left Briar with a neighbor, who was a suspected pedophile, but who was always eager to take care of Briar whenever Donna went on a binge. She was not a misunderstood woman with a drug problem; she was a soulless excuse for a human, who had no desire to change who she was or what she did.

With various drug offenses on her record, Donna was finally sentenced to six years in jail for drug trafficking. The day before her incarceration, she managed to locate the run-down house where Briar's biological father lived. She knocked on the door and told his wife that Briar was Lester's kid, and that they needed to take care of her while she was in the slam. Briar stood stoically on the front stoop, gripping her shabby *Dora the Explorer* thrift shop backpack in one hand and her stuffed *Scooby Doo* toy in the other. Donna leaned forward and pushed Briar through the front door, saying, "I'll be back to get you when I can." That was the last time Briar saw her mother.

When Briar's biological father, the red-headed green-eyed Lester Bush returned home that ening, he was already half drunk and livid with the s tion. For the next few hours, Lester sat on his broke own couch, staring daggers at Briar across the roo s he downed another twelve-pack of Schlitz. This definitely not the reunion Briar had dreamed of so ay having with her natural father. At least she now erstood where her red hair came from. Lester Bush spoke a word to his daughter, and the more he d he meaner he looked. Finally, he yelled at his w "Feed the kid a horse cock sandwich and put her in the basement. I'm sick of looking at her face. I'll track down the bitch's parents in the morning, and they can deal with their sorry ass grandkid." Briar didn't know what horse cock was, but she suddenly realized how very hungry she was, having not eaten since the egg McMuffin she'd split with her mom before coming here. It was now after eight p.m., and she could eat a horse…cock…she guessed.

The sandwich turned out to be a piece of bologna between two slices of Wonder Bread. For the next few days, Lester and his wife fought loudly, while they all treated Briar like the redheaded stepchild she was. Briar slept on a cheap plastic beanbag chair in the cold, damp basement, while being taunted unmercifully by her two half-brother brat siblings, only slightly older than she. On the third day, there was a knock at the door. A dour old woman revealed herself as Briar's maternal grandmother and quickly ushered Briar out of the run-down house, into a beat up old station wagon. Together, they rode in complete silence to the "Home for Little Wanderers."

Life in the orphanage was not bad for Briar, because she felt safe for the first time. Built as an orphanage in 1894, the red brick mansion was located in an affluent neighborhood, with huge old homes on one side, a country club on the other, and an elementary school across the street. Inside there were Boys and Girls dorms, divided up according to age, with approximately twelve beds to a dorm. Briar was placed in the five to ten year-old girls' dorm, which, at the time, had about eight other girls living in it. Younger children were rotated in and out more frequently than the older kids were, because less people seemed to want to adopt or foster those older children. As a result, the dorms housing kids between ten and eighteen years of age were usually filled to capacity. Briar enjoyed being there. Everyone was pretty nice, the food was decent, and there was plenty of it. Good Samaritans donated clothes, books, and toys for the kids. There was nice playground on the property, ensuring that the kids got plenty of exercise. Briar had even made friends with a school classmate named Tammy, who lived just a few houses down. Life was okay, and she would have been content to stay there indefinitely. When couples came to interview or consider a child for adoption, Briar would pull faces, act up, and make herself appear as *unappealing a selection* as she possibly could. It seemed to work, because she was never selected to go home with anyone.

Until two years later…one morning in late November, a man and woman were escorted into the large dining hall, where all the children were having breakfast. The wife was uptight looking, while the husband appeared happy and relaxed as he scanned the room full of children, pointing and commenting to Mrs. Childress, the headmistress of the orphanage, about different kids. As his eyes eventually came to rest on Briar, she lowered her head, shoveling food into her mouth as quickly as she could. The couple and Mrs. Childress walked over to the table and sat down opposite Briar. Mrs. Childress said, "Briar, this is Mr. and Mrs. Jenkins…they'd like to consider taking you to 'foster.' They have another foster child, Amanda, who you might remember was living here when you first joined us. The Jenkins think Amanda would benefit from having another girl in the house to interact with. They have a lovely home, where I think you would be happy and comfortable living. Briar jerked her head up, spitting her mouthful of food back out onto her plate, as she said, "I don't want to go anywhere; I'm happy living here until my mom comes back to get me, Mrs. Childress." With that, Briar stormed out of the dining hall and back to her dorm room. Less than an hour later, Briar was securely strapped in the backseat of a blue Jeep Cherokee, heading to her new foster home with Bud and Leona Jenkins.

In spite of her reluctance, life with the Jenkins appeared as though it wouldn't be too unpleasant for Briar. Although Mrs. Jenkins was still rather aloof and cool, Mr. Jenkins, who insisted on being called Uncle Bud, was very attentive and playful with both girls. It was a comfortable home—certainly the nicest Briar had ever lived in. More importantly, it was still in the same school district, so Briar would not have to switch, and would still see her friend Tammy on a regular basis.

Briar shared a room with Amanda, a sulky overweight seven year-old, who hoarded food and candy under her mattress. Briar only vaguely remembered Amanda from when she first arrived at the orphanage. Their bedroom was pleasant, with two twin beds topped with brightly colored quilts. The beds were separated by a table with a pink heart-shaped lamp that was also a nightlight. Two, four-drawer matching chests of drawers stood on the wall opposite the foot of their beds, with a bookcase holding books and games centered between the two chests. Briar stuck her little suitcase, stuffed with orphanage-donated clothing, beneath her bed, instead of unpacking it into the drawers intended for her…just in case she had to make a speedy departure, she reminded herself.

The family had a cute little dust-mop of a dog named Daisy. On Briar's second day there, Uncle Bud brought her a bicycle with training wheels, since Briar had never ridden a bike before. It was teal, with white streamers hanging from the handle grips, and a white plastic basket attached to the front of the handlebars. Amanda's bike was red, and it had no training wheels. Briar did not like the idea of that, so she spent the next few days teaching herself to ride—first with, but quickly without, the training wheels. Daisy the dog sat perched in the basket, while the two happily cruised around the neighborhood, up one sidewalk and down another.

Being Thanksgiving week, there was no school, and a big family dinner was planned at the Jenkins' home. It would be the first Thanksgiving that Briar had ever spent in a home setting like this, with all of the food, fixings, and potential festivities surrounding it. Briar almost felt excited as she and Amanda helped Mrs. Jenkins prepare the house for company. Together, they cut out turkeys from colored construction paper, making festive decorations as centerpieces for the long harvest table. They put out place settings for twelve people—all coming to meet Briar for the very first time.

After getting into their PJs and ready for bed, Briar and Amanda sat on the fur shag rug separating their beds, playing with the new Barbie dolls Uncle Bud had given them earlier that day. Briar's doll had red hair, an orange mini-dress, and orange boots, while Amanda's had a blonde ponytail, a pink strapless dress, and high gold heels. Neither girl had ever had a Barbie doll before, and both were thrilled. They talked animatedly about accessories they'd like to get for their dolls. It was the happiest Briar had seen Amanda since she'd moved in. Amanda was usually reserved—almost secretive. As they played, Briar overheard Amanda whispering something to her doll that sounded like, "*I hope he doesn't come tonight*."

A few minutes later, Mrs. Jenkins, who preferred to be called Mrs. Jenkins, hollered down the hall, "Lights out, girls, big day tomorrow." Briar reached up and pulled the chain on the nightstand lamp, switching it to nightlight mode—providing just enough glow to use the bathroom if they needed to. They each tucked their doll in beside them, and Briar pulled her stinky *Scooby Doo* doll underneath the covers too. With the lights out, the clock radio on the bedside table projected the time onto the ceiling. It was 9:05 as Briar closed her eyes and drifted off to sleep, happily thinking about turkey, pumpkin pie, Barbie Dolls, and bicycles.

Later that night, a visit to the girls' bedroom by Uncle Bud changed everything...and Briar's hope for a new home and family came crashing down around her ears once again.

Briar raised such a ruckus fighting off Uncle Bud's advances that she woke Mrs. Jenkins, who came crashing through the bedroom door with Daisy the dog right on her heels. Flipping on the overhead light, Mrs. Jenkins saw Briar standing in the middle of her bed, wielding *Scooby Doo* like a weapon. Mr. Jenkins was backing away from Briar, as he stammered out something about checking on the girls. Up popped Amanda too, with a panicked look on her face. Mrs. Jenkins reached up and grabbed Briar by the arm, yanking her off the bed. "You are a trouble-making, little piece of trash like your mother, aren't you?" she hissed. “You’ll go back to the orphanage first thing tomorrow!”

After the couple left Amanda and Briar alone in their room together for what would be the last time, the girls heard raised voices coming from the bedroom down the hall. Briar was still so shaken that Amanda came and sat beside her on the bed. She put her chubby little arm around Briar’s shoulders, as she said under her breath, “I’m sorry I pretended to be asleep, Briar—I just hate him so much, and it hurts more every time he does…what …he…does.” Amanda sobbed.”

Briar still couldn’t stop thinking about what Mrs. Jenkins had said. Had it been her fault what nearly happened? Was it because of her red bright red hair? She suddenly had an idea, and she quickly enlisted Amanda’s help to search through the bathroom cabinets and find what they needed to implement Briar’s plan to change how people saw her. Amanda cried softly as they worked together, cutting off Briar’s massive mane of copper locks and flushing it down the toilet. Then, they shaved off her remaining hair, down to her bare scalp. Briar reached up and touched Amanda's swollen face, assuring her that they would find a way to get her out of there too.

Thanksgiving morning at the crack of dawn, Mrs. Jenkins threw a bald-headed Briar and her meager belongings into the back seat of the Jeep, delivering her back to the "Home for Little Wanderers." Briar overheard Mrs. Jenkins tell Mrs. Childress that Briar was an incorrigible little trollop, and that they wanted nothing more to do with her. After Mrs. Jenkins left, Mrs. Childress quietly put her hand on Briar's shoulder as she led her back to her the young girls' dorm room. Briar, still strikingly beautiful with her huge eyes and alabaster skin, looked up defiantly at Mrs. Childress saying, "You don't know what goes on in that house." Thinking that she would surely get a harsh punishment, Briar was shocked when, instead, Mrs. Childress said, "Now…let's go get you some breakfast and show off your new hairdo to the rest of the kids."

Once Mrs. Childress had deposited Briar in the dining hall, she walked quickly back to her office. During her eighteen years at the orphanage, she had seen and heard it all. She believed that ninety-nine percent of the time, the problem was not with the children; it was with the adults. Perhaps she would request the assistance of a particular social worker she knew to investigate the squeaky-clean living situation at the Jenkins' household.

Word spread quickly that Briar was back at the orphanage. A few hours later, her friend Tammy showed up bearing an invitation from her mom to come have Thanksgiving with their family and a sleepover with Tammy. When Tammy saw Briar's freshly shorn-head, she knew immediately something bad had happened. After getting permission from Mrs. Childress to go with Tammy, Briar threw her PJs and *Scooby Doo* into an old Walmart sack, and the girls headed down the street to the Lerner home.

Mrs. Lerner greeted them at the door with a fresh batch of chocolate chip cookies. Jackie Lerner was the plump Jewish mother Briar secretly wished she'd had. Mrs. Lerner didn't have a job, so she was there to see Tammy off in the morning, and always there to greet her in the afternoon when she got home from school, with snacks and corned beef sandwiches on the best Jewish rye bread. Jackie Lerner was a little concerned about her daughter's close relationship with Briar, not so much because Briar was a Gentile, but because she could only imagine the life and abuse she'd been exposed to prior to life at the orphanage. No doubt she had experienced things children her age should not see, and knowing that past experiences often manifest themselves in other ways, she knew she would have to monitor the relationship closely. Fortunately, Tammy was a child wise beyond her age, and she seemed to have real affection for little Briar. Mrs. L, as the kids called her, was surprised by Briar's shaven head when she walked through the door, but decided not to mention it. Perhaps there had been a lice outbreak at the orphanage…who could know? She was sure Briar would tell Tammy what was going on, and later, Tammy would share it with her mother.

Briar followed Tammy upstairs to her bedroom, newly painted in her favorite shade of lavender. A big white canopy bed stood in the center of the room, laden with stuffed animals and pillows. On the wall opposite the bed, Tammy had a dressing table with a green organdy skirt around it and a large white oval mirror above it. Briar longed to have her own dressing table someday, as she watched Tammy sitting there brushing her thick chestnut hair with one of the many brushes lying on the mirrored glass top. Briar threw her sack in the corner and flopped down on the bed, while Tammy sampled a new assortment of miniature bottles of perfume she'd gotten for her ninth birthday last week. Smell this, Briar, it's called Organza; I think it smells like you. Here, take it, put it in your bag…I want you to have it. Tammy liked something called Tommy Girl, saying she would change the "o" to an "a," and for the next hour they played, happily spraying the different fragrances on each other, and on Scooby Doo too. Tammy's Dad, "Oscar the Grouch," as everyone affectionately called him (his name was Oscar) told them that they "smelled like a couple of "French whores," when they came down later for dinner. Everyone laughed, but neither Tammy nor Briar really got the reference.

After an enjoyable Thanksgiving dinner with the Lerner family and some relatives who'd driven up from Kansas City, Briar and Tammy helped Jackie clear the table and cut up the pies for desert. Briar liked being there, and appreciated that no one made mention all day of her bald head, not that they weren't curious, she could tell. She'd made her mind up that she would tell Tammy the truth about what had happened with Bud Jenkins later…after everyone was in bed, and when no one could hear what they were whispering about.

The next day, Friday, after Briar went back to the orphanage, Tammy did share with her mom what Briar told her happened in the foster home. She had carefully crossed her fingers under the covers when Briar made her promise not to tell anyone. Tammy knew this was something an adult needed to hear about. Jackie was infuriated by the story and spent the next few hours making phone calls to various people, including Mrs. Childress, who was already following up on her own suspicions about the Jenkins family.

Jackie was also attempting to track down a woman named Sarah Barrett, whom she'd met in nursing school years before. They'd lost touch over the years, but she remembered hearing through another classmate that Sarah had married a guy named Malone, and they lived somewhere in Kansas City. Jackie thought of this woman specifically because Sarah, also a striking redhead, had talked about adopting, thinking she possibly could not have children due to a tipped uterus. Not knowing what the outcome of that was, Jackie was determined to find Sarah and, just possibly, convince Sarah and her husband to consider Briar.

She needed to get this precious child out of the "system," and into a healthy home, before any further damage was done to her. Briefly, she'd considered adopting Briar herself, but they were Orthodox Jews, and she knew she'd be better off raised in a Christian home. Meanwhile, she and Oscar would see to it that this Jenkins family was brought to task for what had occurred in their home, and make certain that they were never allowed to foster another child.

Exactly 136 days later, on Briar's ninth birthday, April 13, 1995, Briar's adoption by Sarah and Mike Malone was official. As the whole family stood in the kitchen of the modest home in the Northland subdivision called Countryside, Briar bent forward to blow out the candles on her *Scooby Doo* birthday cake. She had outgrown *Scooby Doo* by now, but she didn't care—it was the thought that counted, and she had never had a store-bought birthday cake with her name on it in her entire life. At that very moment, her new cousin, Wesley, walked through the front door holding a bouquet of multi-colored Gerber Daisies. Briar's eyes lit up when she saw Wesley, who had become her best friend and constant companion over the five-month long adoption screening process, during which time the Barretts were allowed to foster Briar. So began a life-long tradition of Wesley sending Briar Gerber Daisies every year on her birthday—no matter where in the world she was.

Chapter 2

Present Day

The volcanic stepping-stones were wet and slippery from the constant spray of water flowing over Sacred Falls. For an eternity of time, the falls had poured millions of gallons of fresh water daily over the jagged lava lip of the falls in a never-ending cascade of icy water and mini rainbows. The sparkling clear water tumbled down 150 feet into a large volcanic bowl, worn smooth by time. The pool was believed to be a sacred spot by the locals, who would gather with baskets of fruit as offerings to a maiden and her young lover, believed in legend to have been murdered by her husband for an adulterous affair. The husband discovered the lovers in an amorous embrace and stabbed them both in the heart. Then he threw them over the falls, where their broken bodies eventually disappeared, but their spirits remained in the pool. The legend had been passed down for centuries, one generation after the next, embellished with each telling. The beautiful maiden was made more beautiful, and the lover ever more handsome, until the couple was elevated to mystical symbols of tragic love.

The water moved on after a brief pause in the pool, where it swirled gently in a circular motion, then spilled over the pool's rim and flowed downhill in a fast running stream into the turbulent ocean on Oahu's North Shore.

The stone steps, cut and set centuries before, were treacherous for even the most nimble visitor to the famous park. The man carrying the body over his shoulders moved cautiously, placing one foot firmly on the next stone before taking the next step. Moonlight filtered through the triple canopy of tropical fauna, casting ghostly shadows that swayed in the breeze. The roar of the falls masked the man's labored breathing and occasional curse when he would lose his footing. Near the top, he slipped and fell. The body landed on top of him in an awkward position, the head flopped loosely from the broken neck, and the dead man's eyes, locked wide in death, bore into the killer's face inches away.

"Not yet, my pretty," he said, and pushed the body away.

He stood, wiping his hands on his pant legs, then reached again for the body. Two-hundred pounds of dead weight should not have been difficult for the killer to handle, and yet he found himself straining to get it up and over his shoulder once again.

"Too much slacking off," he mumbled.

His well-muscled body was the result of years of training and time spent in the gym; nevertheless, age has a way of fighting back and stealing a man's stamina. With the body once again held securely, he started back up the pathway stairs. At the top was an overlook platform, with guardrails and danger signs warning not to lean over the railings, posted every few feet, extending out over the falls. With a shrug, he let the body fall to the deck. He bent, took the shoes and socks off, emptied the man's pockets, and placed everything inside the shoes. He dug into his cargo pocket and chuckled as he withdrew a small flash drive.

“Dumb bitch will definitely take the fall for this,” he said.

He flipped the computer flash drive in the air, smiling at the memory of the stick’s contents. Not his cup of tea, but damning nonetheless. The dozens of photos showed the dead man lounging around a hotel room, nude and definitely aroused. Other photos included a voluptuous young woman, also nude, in various erotic positions. The flash drive was an indictment of adultery for the man; for the woman, perhaps just a keepsake of a fun summer, spent with a handsome married man in Hawaii.

Unfortunately, the last time the two were together, they had argued about her staying in Hawaii instead of returning to California, where she had recently relocated from the Big Apple.

"Sorry, Craig, I have a career, and so do you. You also have a wife from one of the most influential families in Hawaii. We both knew what we were getting into when we started this affair. It's not going to work for us on a 'forever' basis. You can visit me in California, but I'm not going to stay and become your island *wahine*."

"But, I've fallen in love with you, Briar. If you stay I will divorce Kalani. You and I are so good together baby, and even if you won't say it, I know you love me." Craig said.

"Of course I've loved being with you these past few weeks Craig, but I'm not officially 'in love' with you. I can't, no, I won't alter my life…or yours this drastically. Go home to your wife and your real life, and let me pack." Briar said, realizing as those words spilled out, just how callous she must sound. That's not how she really felt, but she knew she wasn't ready for this bit a commitment yet.

Craig's demeanor changed drastically, as he grabbed Briar by the shoulders and shoved her backwards into a chair. Go ahead and leave then, you cold bitch. This was just a few weeks of cheap sex for me too baby, and honestly…I've had better!"

Briar bristled as Craig turned and started for the door, "That's really a douche bag thing to say, and you don't mean it!" On impulse, she reached into her purse lying on the table next to the chair, grabbing the flash drive, then hurling it across the room at Craig. "Here," Briar snapped, "Go refresh your memory, asshole. When you grow up, maybe we'll talk. Meanwhile, get the hell out of here with your juvenile attitude!"

Briar immediately regretted flinging the drive at him, but Craig caught it mid-flight, leaving the hotel room immediately, and slamming the door behind him. He had more to lose than she did if those pictures ever got out, so Briar wasn't too worried. Besides, she'd get the flash drive back once he cooled down and came to his senses.

Of course, the killer didn't know these details, or how the USB drive came to be in Craig Stanton's possession. He only knew that he was paid to kill the man and make it look like a suicide. This was easy money; suicides were an easy set up. You kill the target, leave a note behind, or other evidence scattered around the scene, and collect your paycheck. His real motivation, however, was not the money, nor the promise of more business to come from his patron. No, his motivation came from a darker place in his mind. It was a primal place, a bloodlust place…he needed to kill. When he looked into his victim's eyes and saw the fear, and the last flicker of life, it gave him such a euphoric release that it left him momentarily faint. The need for this release was coming more frequently with each new kill. He knew that he would be out of control someday, but meanwhile, he would continue…with or without his patron's permission.

He stuck the drive in one of the victim's shoes, and then placed the wallet on top of it, where it was sure to be found. From his other cargo pocket, he took out a Ziploc baggy; inside was a dead gecko. He opened the baggy, held it to his nose, and inhaled the rich sweet scent of decay deep into his lungs. He pried the victim's mouth open wide with his hand, and forced the carcass down the throat. Using his index finger, he shoved it as deep as he could. When he withdrew his finger, he placed it in his mouth and sucked…savoring the taste. Tears spilled from his eyes, ran down his cheeks, and he whimpered. This was not part of the plan; it was his own little contribution to the tableau.

"I loved you, Dee. Why did you treat me that way…why, why?" he cried.

After a moment, a steely resolve replaced his tortured features, and he was in control again. Satisfied that the evidence was in place, he raised the man by lifting him under the arms. Once he had him upright, he gave the man one last look, letting the dead face burn itself into his memory bank. He opened his mouth and kissed the corpse as deep as his tongue would go. After a moment, he pulled away, releasing a small whimper. With uncommon strength, he lifted the body and threw it over the railing. He watched as the body disappeared into the raging water, and then hurried down the hill to report to his patron that all had gone according to plan.

The rushing water swallowed up the body immediately. It began to tumble wildly, hitting and slamming into razor sharp outcroppings and jagged lava. By the time it landed in the pool, it was mutilated and unrecognizable, with every major bone broken or fractured. Even so, it didn't take the Honolulu coroner long to identify the body the next day as that of Craig Stanton…popular three-term senator from the great State of Hawaii. It also didn't take the Honolulu homicide division long to zero in on one particular suspect either. They weren't buying the cause of death as suicide. The flash drive told a much more revealing reason why Stanton was dead.

Chapter 3

Briar Malone stood transfixed in her Marina Del Rey apartment overlooking the acres of sailboats, powerboats, and fishing boats in the harbor below, as she watched the news reports about the suicide death of Senator Craig Stanton. The CNN, MSNBC and FOX talking heads were using it as their lead story on the six o'clock news hour. The cable channels had their reporters on the ground in Oahu, spewing out details as fast as they could make them up. They had five minutes of airtime to fill, so if there were not enough facts to report…then they just winged it. The FOX reporter was the first to report that maybe there was more to the death than just a suicide.

"Based on un-named sources inside the Oahu homicide division, there might have been foul play involved. A certain female suspect was being sought for questioning."

A kaleidoscopic-reel of images of her with Craig flashed across Briar's mind, as she struggled to keep her emotions in check. . In shock, she flopped down on an overstuffed ottoman, riveted to the broadcast, as the reporter repeated the suspicion that the cause of death was not suicide, but perhaps a lover's quarrel ending in murder…

"Reliable un-named sources within the HPD have disclosed that a flash drive, containing explicit photos of Senator Stanton with a young woman in a hotel room had been found at the scene. The source indicated that the unidentified woman was being sought for questioning, but was not a suspect at this time. We will keep you updated as things develop; back to you, Bret…"

Briar was surprised at the mixed feelings of guilt, alarm and remorse—all unfamiliar sensations for this hard-shelled little cookie. She rolled her head from side to side, in an attempt to shake off these bad feelings. She knew she didn't have anything to do with Craig's death…how could she? She was in L.A. at the time of death, here in her apartment—end of story. But the fear crept back in. If it was suicide, was it because of her and the way things ended when she departed Oahu three weeks ago?

She knew Craig had fallen hard for her in the month they had spent nearly every waking moment together. Even with his re-election campaign ramping up, he still managed to spend most days and nights with her. Briar didn't believe the suicide scenario for one second. Craig was too much of an egotist to end his own life. He was rich, having married into old Island money, he was very popular, and he was well known throughout Hawaii for his hard work in Washington to bring the pork back home. And, most importantly, Briar knew early-on that Craig had deep-rooted issues and doubts about his manhood.

These issues came to the surface more than once during their love making, when he would just burst into tears. The first time it happened, she was alarmed, but she calmed him down with soothing whispers and gestures of understanding. In spite of these unusual bouts of behavior, Briar enjoyed the sex and their love making. She had no hang ups when it came to her own satisfaction, and enjoyed sex even more when 'love' was not part of the equation. Craig had skillfully fulfilled those needs, and provided that sweet release for her…crying jags aside.

Chapter 4

The real purpose of Briar's trip to the Islands two months earlier had been more a favor than a real urge to go, and for sure not to have an illicit affair with a married man. Her Aunt Cydny owned a penthouse near Diamond Head, and had asked Briar to fly over and check on it…and on Briar's cousin, Wesley.

Wesley Barrett lived in the penthouse more or less year round. Although, he was known to disappear for a few months at a time, whenever he and his partner argued and he needed to get away. Briar and Wesley (born just four days apart) grew up more like brother and sister than cousins, following Briar's adoption into the family at nine years of age. Inseparable from that point on, they fought each other's battles, wore each other's clothes, and kept each other's secrets. Briar even knew Wesley was gay before he did. Their glamorous Aunt Cydny, was like a second mother to Briar and Wesley growing up, schooling them both in how to act and dress. She nicknamed Briar

"Bribaby" and Wesley was her "Precious Angel." Cydny thought them to be so much alike, she joked that Wesley was Briar with a dick.

Wesley's father (Cyd's brother), was the charismatic, womanizing racecar driver Chandler Barrett, who made millions designing and building state-of-the-art racecar engines. Chan died years earlier in a fiery crash, setting a world speed record at the Bonneville Salt Flats. His fortune was split between his sons, Adam and Wesley. Wesley decided to enjoy his portion of the fruits of Chan's labor, by living like a trust fund baby…at least for a few years.

Aunt Cyd had called Briar a few weeks earlier, pleading, "Bribaby, just go there and make sure Wesley hasn't destroyed the place. I'm snowed under in New York, helping Piper prepare her new collection for Fashion Week. I'll ship you some Piper Marie runway samples when we're done. She has come far since her teenage internship with the girls and me at Designs on You. She's a better clothing designer than I ever was." Cyd stopped long enough to take a breath, then continued.

"Go relax and play with Wesley for a few weeks. You need a break anyway, after the craziness you were involved in last year with the FBI and that pervert at their Academy trying to kill you. Take some time to sort things out. What better place to do it than my old tropical stomping grounds?"

"Sure, I'll go, Auntie. How can I refuse such an appealing invitation? I don't really need any 'downtime,' though, and that 'pervert,' as you call him, didn't try to kill me…he just forced himself on me. Actually, I feel bad about how seriously I injured the jerk. He won't try running his hand up another woman's skirt without considering the consequences again." Briar winced at the memory of putting her senior instructor in the hospital with multiple broken bones, lacerations, and a very swollen pair of nuts. "I'm worried about Cousin Wesley anyway. I've called him numerous times, but keep getting his recording, and he hasn't returned any of my calls."

"That's certainly out of character for Wesley," Cyd said. "Let me know what the ticket costs and I'll wire you the money. You need to send me your new banking information anyway, so I can have Arturo's people fill it with whatever you need."

"I'm afraid to ask, Auntie, but who is Arturo?"

"Oh, just a man, sweetheart…someone to play with until the right one comes around."

Briar laughed as she stared at her iPhone, which had suddenly gone dead. Aunt Cyd was one of the best people in Briar's world, if a bit eccentric. She was still wild and glamorous after countless marriages and *arrangements* as Auntie called them. Auntie C had done so much for Briar over the years, never questioning, never judging, always supportive. Briar could never refuse her anything.

The following day, Briar was jetting across the Pacific, sitting in first class on Hawaiian Airlines. The five-hour flight from L.A.X. to Honolulu was uneventful, other than for formulating a plan to hook up with an old boyfriend from the University of Missouri, Cody Bentley. Cody had moved to Oahu shortly after graduation, to work for the Department of Defense as an engineer on a missile-tracking program. Briar had retained a fondness for Cody through the years, and was looking forward to seeing him again. Who knows? Maybe it would turn into something 'real.' Timing is everything, and after the drama and trauma of the last few years, she was ready to settle in somewhere, and what better place, truly, than Hawaii? It wasn't meant to be. A day after her arrival on Oahu, Cody was reassigned to Nome Alaska for some kind of missile tracking calibration mumbo-jumbo, and would be gone for several months.

Briar arrived at Honolulu International at 5:10, hailed a cab, and rode in rush-hour traffic the familiar five-mile route to Auntie's prestigious Gold Coast condo, located between Waikiki and Diamond Head. Forty-five minutes later, Briar found Wesley "alive and safe" in the apartment, but in a major funk over suspicions that Porter, his lover for the past two years, was seeing a sous-chef at the Royal Hawaiian.

"Snap out of it, Angel," Briar said. "Porter adores you, and besides, he's twenty-five years your senior. If anyone should be cheating on the relationship, it should be you. Let's go for a ride and maybe find you a little *local boy action* of your own."

Delighted to see Briar, who was the only person who could change his mood in an instant, Wesley followed obediently as she grabbed a ring of keys off the kitchen pantry door, and took the elevator to the underground parking lot. She immediately spotted Aunt Cyd's 1977 yellow Corvette, slid off the car cover, stashed the T-Tops in the back, and cranked it up. Wesley had his own classic 1969 red Corvette parked in the next stall, but Briar had always preferred driving this one. Wesley offered, but as usual, Briar took the helm.

With screeching tires on the garage's painted floor, she maneuvered her way up the ramp and out onto Diamond Head Road. As always, the day was filled with plenty of sunshine, a balmy trade wind, and the rich scent of tropical flowers. February was her favorite month in Hawaii. She cruised down Kahala Avenue, taking a left on Kealaolu, and a right onto Kalanianaole Highway toward KoKo Head and Hawaii Kai. Traffic was always heavy on Kalanianaole, but this time of day, it was almost at a standstill. She wasn't unaware, either, of all the looks she was getting from the men…and women. She was beautiful, and knew it. Her red hair blowing in the wind, the large Dior sunglasses perched on her face, and her friendly smile never ceased to attract. Wesley was equally handsome, so the two of them in a neon yellow Corvette was a sight to behold. After an hour in traffic to go seven miles, she hit open road and gunned it towards Hanauma Bay.

The ride was exhilarating for the pair, and helped clear their heads. Parked on the ridge overlooking the Bay, the pair watched the snorkeling tourists as they caught each other up on their lives. On the way back, they stopped at KoKo Marina for shave ices at Kokonuts.

Back on H-1 heading toward Waikiki, Wesley suggested they go to Ala Moana Center to pick up a platinum bracelet he'd ordered for Porter's birthday the following week. "If I find out for certain that old queen is cheating on me, I'll keep the bracelet myself."

While Wesley went into Royal Jewelry, Briar did some window-shopping. Out of the corner of her eye, she spotted a tall, handsome man, walking amidst a crowd of people. She moved closer to see what the attraction was. The moment she made eye contact with Craig Stanton, she knew how she would be spending (at least part of) her Hawaiian vacation. Two days later, Briar was engaged in a sexual romp with Senator Craig Stanton in a suite at the Royal Hawaiian Hotel in

Waikiki…provided by his re-election S-PAC money machine.

Chapter 5

Her attention was drawn back to the present when a crescendo of music blared out, indicating "breaking news." Briar hated the shrill notes of alarm with the clacking teletype in the background. It was more suited to an incoming ICBM warning than a dinnertime attention grabber.

On the screen, an obviously distraught woman was standing under an umbrella in a heavy downpour. Someone out of sight was holding the umbrella protectively over her as she dabbed at her eyes in apparent grief.

"...I know she must be involved somehow with Craig's death. Who else could it be? The moment I discovered the photos, I knew they weren't real. Craig would never do that to me. He has never even looked at another woman in the twenty years we have been married..."

"Excuse me, Mrs. Stanton, Hector Rodriguez with CNN. You believe this to be part of

a smear campaign, by your husband's opponent running for his seat in the Senate...?"

"*Of course it is,*" *she snapped.* "*Why else would they bring in a mainland whore to 'set Craig up' in that hotel room? He was obviously drugged; any idiot can see that. I think the whole thing was arranged to look like blackmail. Craig told me that there were unusual things occurring and that he'd had threatening calls demanding large sums in return for not releasing those disgusting photos. I think Craig refused to be pulled into such shenanigans, and his opponent chose the only other option to get Craig out of the race...*"

"*Are you saying that you believe Sammy Hinoko had your husband murdered just to get him out of the race?*"

"*Yes, I am saying that. Sammy Hinoko and his family have done far worse things in the Islands over the years, the least of which is that 'land grab' on the Big Island, which made them millions. I'm not saying Sammy did it personally; I'm suggesting that he was behind it. The Mainland woman was probably who pushed Craig over the falls."* She sobbed into a damp hanky, then continued.

"I have talked personally with Mayor Hilo about this, and he agrees with me. Find that woman, and we will find out who killed my husband."

Briar started to feel panic, knowing that it wouldn't take the Honolulu police long to come up with her name and notify the LAPD to pick her up as a suspect in a murder. She was innocent; there was no way that she could be tied to the murder on Oahu. However, she also knew from her brief stint at the FBI's school at Quantico what arrest procedures were for murder suspects.

This would necessarily be a federal crime because Craig was a sitting U.S. Senator, so his murder fell under their jurisdiction. This took things to an even higher level. She would be caught in the middle of a tug of war between the FBI and the HPD. Not only would she be bounced around between the two agencies, the whole affair could turn into a three-ring media circus with her being the lady fired out of the cannon.

An uproar for a quick conviction would thunder out of the senatorial chambers for the murder of one of their own. Killing a member of Congress was tantamount to assassination, and by God, that just wouldn't go unpunished. Priority would be demanded, and "the accused" (her) made an example of to the good folks back home.

Briar ran herself a glass of water and sipped thoughtfully. The last thing she was going to do was to let herself be taken in and paraded before the country as a murder suspect. Her short time at Quantico taught her how the system worked, and how it favored the good old-boy network; they would protect their own. In spite of being head of her class, she was booted out three months into a four month course for reporting a senior instructor for unwanted sexual advances. Never mind that she almost beat the man to death for his effort to get his hand up her skirt; she was found to be too aggressive in defending herself and handed her walking papers.

Briar Malone was a survivor. She had learned very early in life how to take care of herself against the system. She had been through terrible experiences as a child. They had hardened her and taught her never to let her guard down. On the surface, she was an intelligent, caring, compassionate woman. However, anyone who "crossed the line," did so at their own peril.

No way was she going to be a media star, or a victim of the system ever again, she thought defiantly.

She was getting hungry—a common reaction when she was under stress. She pulled a paper plate off the stack in the pantry and a loaf of wheat bread from the top of the fridge. The refrigerator came with the apartment. It was one of those thirty-cubic foot whiz-bang stainless monstrosities that made crushed ice, cubed ice, and shaved ice for snow cones. It was also big enough to freeze a cow in if she so desired, which she didn't. Briar rolled her eyes at having forgotten to pick up a bottle of grape syrup at the market to make her favorite flavored shave ice. The treat was her only concession to going off her fitness program, other than for the occasional Baskin Robins chocolate shake. Inside the fridge, she found a pack of deli meat that had begun to curl around the edges and a couple of mustard packets she'd saved from In-N-Out Burger. She tore the mustard packs open and squeezed them onto the bread. Then, carefully, she began to tear off the dried edges from around the deli meat. In the process, she sniffed the meat and gagged. She turned the slice in her hand over; it was gray and oily. Wrinkling her nose, Briar disgustedly tossed the meat and bread into the trash. Back in the fridge, she found an open can of Slim Fast, smelled it, shrugged, and drank it.

In the three months she had lived in the Marina City Club, she had not missed a morning of working out in the Club's gym. She had met many of the women residents in her Pilates classes, and several of the men in the building where in her weight training classes took place. The news had traveled fast that a hot redhead was working out every morning, and attendance had skyrocketed among the male residents. Briar was used to the attention, and basically ignored it, which made her even more of an attraction to the stud wannabes. She learned at an early age how to use her beauty and wit to her advantage. The world was a tough place, and Briar knew her way around it. It was all just a part of her survival.

The few large things she owned, she had shipped from New York to L.A. That was three months ago, and the shipment was apparently lost somewhere between Hoboken and Little Rock. Her apartment came furnished, so it really didn't matter if the shipment ever turned up or not. It was insured, and at the moment was the least of her worries. Since arriving in L.A. she had picked up a few cases of fraud investigation for insurance agencies, which paid well enough to cover her expenses with some left over. Word was getting around about her experience and competence, and she'd recently landed a couple of big payday accounts, tracking and recovering stolen jewelry and personal items. These were usually wealthy clients, who preferred not to get the police involved due to unwanted publicity. Instead, the clients left it up to their legal counsel to resolve. Briar didn't mind doing these types of cases; there was very little danger involved, no clock to punch, and they always paid well. After three years of being a case investigator for several different New York law firms, followed by her short-lived FBI gig, she was ready for a slower life. She needed to be out of the high-threat inner-city world, where each case seemed to pull her into life-ending situations.

Now, her new slower life was being threatened. She was a potential murder suspect that the Feds and the Honolulu PD would soon sniff out, appearing with badges held high and loud voices screaming out her Miranda rights from a laminated card. She wasn't going to sit around and wait for those things to unfold. She rummaged through her bag for her cell phone and hit a speed-dial number.

It took less than a second for the signal to bounce up to the communications satellite, sitting in a stationary position twenty-five thousand miles overhead, and bounce down to Oahu.

On the second ring, it was answered.

"I'm not talking to you, Briar Malone."

"Wesley, don't you hang up on me again. I told you I was sorry and that I had to come home early. I picked up a new case and needed to get back to L.A. quickly—I swear it."

"Is that when you kicked Porter out of the apartment before you left? The man was left homeless, Briar. God, have you no knowledge of what life is like on the street over here? Porter could have been killed…or worse."

Worse than death? Briar rolled her eyes, not wanting to go there with Wesley.

"I gave Porter five hundred dollars to hold him over until he received his paycheck. I wouldn't exactly call that being homeless."

"Porter doesn't understand money. Why do you think he depends on me to take care of him?"

"Let me guess…could it be because you have a lot of money and Porter is more cunning than you think he is? Or is it that Auntie's apartment is quite a cut above the grass shack you found him in? Christ, the man is a freeloader, Wesley; you need to dump him," Briar said in an exasperated tone.

"I can't, Briar—I love him. As long as there is a breath in my body, Porter will always have a home. And not to put too fine a point on it, the Grass Shack was an upscale restaurant where he was the head chef, so stop being so bitchy."

"Whatever, drama queen! I think you're just getting bored with this whole trust fund baby life. Why else would you, (a male version of me) become so obsessed with a guy twenty-five years your senior, when you could have your choice of any gay guy on the island? Unless you have so lost your self-confidence by sitting on your nuts 'luxuriating' for the past few years. Maybe it's time for you to get your confidence and manhood back again by doing something meaningful and worthy of your many talents. A life of surfing and sunning doesn't do much to enhance the 'big brain on Brad,' now does it, Angel?" Briar threw in a line from their favorite movie *Pulp Fiction*.

"How did you get so fricking smart?" Wesley laughed, "You're only four days older than me."

"You mean older than I. Why am I still having to correct your English after all these years? You forget—I'm adopted. Perhaps I came from a deeper gene pool than you did—ever think of that?"

"Not likely, Briar—I think you were the lone star of that gene pool," Wesley quipped. "By adopting you, our family saved you from the unimaginable indignity of going through life with your biological father's last name. Do you really think you would have survived high school, college, and the FBI Academy with the name Briar Bush?" Wesley laughed hysterically.

Wesley's laughter got Briar going too, breaking the tension. "As though it wasn't hard enough for me in the orphanage being called the *briar bush* because of my hair—and that was by little kids that didn't even know the alternate meaning yet." By this time, they were both rolling.

"You should literally get on your knees every day and give thanks to the gods that the Malones took pity on your little red-headed ass and saved you from a fate worse than death," howled Wesley.

As the laughing began to subside, Wesley said, "Before I forget, how did all those miles get put on Auntie's car? Did it just drive the crap out of its self while I was on Maui? Did it just happen to park itself in long term parking at HNL on the exact same day you left the Island?"

"As long as we are talking about the Vette, which belongs to Auntie, not you or me…it was a wedding gift from Uncle Duane, and she obviously loves that car more than she loved Uncle Duane—because she's still married to it," Briar joked.

"All I remember is that she left Uncle Duane for some broke-dick young guy," Wesley recalled. "Poor Duane worshipped Auntie, and was devastated when he caught her cheating with that boy toy."

"I know," said Briar. "She told me once that she would probably still be married to Duane if she hadn't gotten caught. Unfortunately, Uncle Duane lost so much face among the local hoi polloi that he sold all of his holdings here and moved back to the Midwest to lick his deeply inflicted wounds."

"Wesley, can we get serious for a minute? I need your help. I might be in some really big trouble."

Oddly, static played out in the momentary silence as the conversation paused.

"What kind of big trouble?" Wesley's voice was much lower and more concerned than a few moments earlier.

"I'll explain it all to you when I get there. I need for you to meet me my flight…I'll call you once I know my arrival time."

"Briar, I asked what kind of big trouble. Before I agree to anything, I need to know what you're getting me into. I don't need any more trouble in my life at the moment. Porter is having an affair behind my back with a busboy, for God's sake. He comes home at all hours, if at all, smelling of cheap bathhouse soap. I'm afraid he'll bring something home…I'm at my wit's end," he paused to blow his nose. "I'm afraid every time someone rings down in the lobby…thinking it might be the police here to arrest me for all the speeding and parking tickets *someone* got while *I* was out of town. My God, Briar, I may have warrants out for my arrest because of the tickets you racked up…"

"I'm sorry, precious. I'll pay for the tickets and any legal fees when I get there, but I did have fun getting them."

"Briar, knock off the jokes," Wesley said, "This is serious. I could lose my license…maybe even have to spend time in the slam. I'm too damned pretty to survive jail!"

"Angel, if I didn't need your help, I wouldn't ask. We've always fought each other's battles, and you are the one person I know I can truly count on in life. Now, will you help me or not?"

"You know I will, Briar, but not until you tell me what kind of trouble you might be bringing to my door."

Satellite static filled the receivers on both ends…

“I think I’m going to be charged with the murder of Senator Craig Stanton.”

“Holy fucking shit, Briar!”

Chapter 6

Senior Detective, Sergeant Kimo Kanoa of the Honolulu Police Department, sat fidgeting with his pen and notebook. He listened as Frank Thompson, the FBI's special agent sent from Washington, was ticking off the bureau's standard operating procedure of how Senator Stanton's case was going to be run.

"Number three, we work as a team," Thompson said. "And I'm the leader, got it? We locate the woman, read her Miranda, and we sky out of here. Is this understood?" The big *haole* prick ran a finger around his tight collar in an attempt to ease the tropical heat.

"Excuse me, Frank—may I call you Frank?" Kimo asked in a condescending tone. "Until I get further clarification from upstairs, HPD will remain the lead agency on the case."

"I *am* the upstairs. Who do you think sent me?" Thompson said smugly. "Just follow my commands and we'll have this matter cleared up in no time, Sergeant."

Kimo flipped his notebook closed and stood, "I go off shift in a few minutes; let's pick this up in the morning. My son's first *lu'au* is tonight and I can't miss it. We're *pau* here," Kimo said, ending the conversation abruptly and heading for the conference room door.

"Hold it right there, Sergeant Kanoa," Thompson called gruffly. "Uh-uh, sorry, pal. Call Mama and tell her you can't make it tonight. Liberty is canceled until we have this case closed."

Kimo stared at the man for a few moments, turned, and went out the door, closing it softly behind him.

"Get back in here, Sergeant, now, or I'll have you walking a beat at the airport," Thompson yelled.

The squad room fell silent at the disturbance. Kimo made circles with his finger alongside his head, "'*Okole-lolo*," he said, and continued out of the room. The other detectives smiled. Most mainland *haoles* were dumb asses; they all agreed.

Kimo stood out in the fresh air blowing in from the ocean and inhaled the smoke from his cigarette deep into his lungs. One of his few weaknesses was Japanese cigarettes; they were harsh and burned going in and coming out…and he liked that. Mainland smokes were too weak for him, like most things coming over to the Islands. Mainlanders were too complicated; they never slowed down to enjoy the beauty of life and were always so serious about the simplest of things. They always thought they knew the answer before the question was even asked. Take Agent Frank Thompson, for example, he was all worked-up over Senator Stanton's death; he thought he would find the woman, fill out the appropriate forms, and fly back to D.C. to senatorial accolades. Kimo shook his head.

"No, Mr. Special F.B.I Agent, this murder was committed by a sick and dangerous man that

will strike again if I don't stop him soon. There may be a woman in the background, but this murder was committed by a very deranged individual. I've seen his work before."

Kimo prided himself that he could trace his linage back to the ancients that canoed from Tahiti so many centuries ago. His bloodlines were as pure as any Hawaiian could have, and he was proud of it, in his own simple way. His fifteen years with HPD were good years sprinkled with promotions and accommodations for bravery and excellent work. His current assignment to Homicide was no accident. He was a natural investigator and could think through the toughest of cases and then apply basic police footwork to solve them. He was a tenacious investigator and was the only detective in the department to never quit a case until he had it solved. Nothing of his EVER went to the cold-case files. Consequently, he had multiple open cases working at any given time. He didn't have any outside interests, and was virtually on the job all the time. Captain Lee also gave Kimo the tough cases, knowing that if they could be solved, Kimo was his go-to man. The other men in the squad called him *Da Popoki* (The Cat) because of his fearless disregard for his own life when in pursuit of his prey.

He had lied about having a *lu'au* to go to; in fact, he wasn't even married, and had no plans of ever being so. Women were too difficult and he never quite understood their hold over men. Sure, he was a normal man and had his needs, and he had an outlet for them. His landlady, Suki Tashikawa, was more than accommodating. Every month-end, he would add an extra fifty to the rent money and receive a quick tumble on Suki's *tatami* in her downstairs apartment. There was no foreplay or post play…just a quick release, and he was gone. He liked his simple life, living alone in his small apartment close to town. In fact, he didn't even own a car of his own; he took the bus or hitched a ride with a patrol car to take him where he needed to go. Now, he wanted to visit the coroner's lab again. Something was bothering him that itched in the back of his mind. He scratched the back of his head as he started for the coroner's office two blocks away.

The sharp, tangy smell of formaldehyde hit Kimo as he entered through the back door of Hawaii's large crime lab. The ground floor was dedicated to the coroner and his gruesome work, with a cold storage area in the basement for what the coroner called his "pit-stop" guests. For most of the dead that came through the morgue, it was usually a brief stay before the family claimed the remains and had it moved to a mortuary. The long-term guests were the homeless or unidentifiable, and were dispatched to the crematorium once their cases were closed.

Kimo swiped at his nose and took the stairs to the second floor where the labs were located. He stopped shortly at the landing, clutching his side.

"*Oh-ho, smokes kapu, Kimo. More betta you stop, bruddah,*" he wheezed.

"Kimo, what you grind?" asked an older man in a lab coat walking toward Kimo as he entered the lab.

"I didn't eat nothing, Uncle (a respectful term for a man who is of your parents' generation). "It's those damned Japanese smokes. They gonna kill me, *bumbai,*" Kimo said.

"Sooner than later is my guess," the coroner said. "Come over here; I have the test results from the other two murders. Very interesting, indeed." George Kau had been the city coroner for thirty-two years. "Indeed" was his favorite word—every conversation would be peppered with it. Kimo had heard him use it hundreds of times over the years; it had become a contest among the police officers to see how many times they could prompt George to say it. Kimo often kept count himself.

Both men stood over the granite lab table peering at three photos. The powdery substance looked the same in each, although one was tinged brown.

"Blood," George said. "The same chemical breakdown as the others, indeed, except for the blood tinted powder."

"Which sample came from Senator Stanton?" Kimo held a thick magnifier to his eye.

"Number three here, the one with the blood stains. I took it from the index and middle fingers of the right hand."

"What is the substance, Uncle?"

"A very common substance indeed, Kimo."

"Indeed?"

"Indeed so…it is sugar, confectioner's sugar, to be precise," he smiled. "Our killer either eats a lot of donuts or he is a cake baker."

The men straightened, looking at each other smiling. Uncle nodded his head knowingly.

"He is a very large man indeed, possibly from sampling his baking all day. Based on the crushed vertebrae in the necks of all three dead men, I have the killer at between two-fifty and three hundred pounds. A very powerful man, indeed."

"Or maybe someone who works in the sugar mills? That could account for the strength, Uncle."

"No, Kimo. This sugar comes to us by way of the mainland…either Texas, Florida, or Louisiana. Our sugar is extracted from cane, and is somewhat course. This sugar comes from sugar beets, and is much finer when processed."

"I am always amazed at the simplest of comparisons, Uncle. Nothing is ever what one would expect."

"Kimo, that is a very astute observation, indeed. Most men never look beyond the obvious. They go through life all the poorer for it."

"Perhaps. Now I have one more favor to ask, Uncle. Can you send this sample off to the National Lab on the Mainland?"

"I am ahead of you this time, Kimo. I have already sent it off. Even so, it will be a while before I receive any results. Indeed, we have very low priority with that Mainland crew."

"Tell them this is urgent; it involves Senator Stanton's death. Say that FBI Special Agent Thompson is requesting it. We'll see if he has as much pull as he thinks he has." Kimo smiled and patted the old man on the shoulder.

"Oh, Kimo, before I forget. You were correct about the room in the photos. It is indeed at the Royal Hawaiian. I sent one of the techs over to compare," Uncle said proudly. "It's the executive suite, room 222."

Kimo smiled, "Very good. I would have guessed the suite on the wing closest to the pool."

"An easy mistake, indeed. Now go, I have work to do."

"Ten 'indeeds' in ten minutes. Could be a new record," Kimo chuckled to himself.

Chapter 7

Wesley parked in metered parking and checked his surroundings before climbing out of his 1969 classic Corvette, careful not to touch the freshly polished red body. Corvettes were a family tradition, starting with his Grandpa Tom getting the first two 1953 Corvettes off the assembly line at the Leeds Chevy plant in Kansas City. He'd seen old photos of those two cars, a white one with red leather interior, and a light blue one with white interior. His dad, Chandler Barrett, had continued the Corvette obsession, owning twelve of them when he died. Wesley chose to keep this particular one, Adam kept three, and the rest were sold at auction. He cherished his "Pretty Little Red Corvette," and named it "Prince." Corvettes were practical in Hawaii, because their fiberglass bodies didn't rust out like every other vehicle on the island.

He pushed his Prada sunglasses higher up his nose and popped the collar up on his Burberry polo before he struck out for the huge terminal.

Satisfied in his mind that he wouldn't stand out too much among the crowds of tourists and visitors thronging the area, he started for the bedlam ahead. One half of the crowd leaving, the other half getting "lei'd" on arrival, making this one of the busiest and most unique airport terminals in the world. He wished he'd known the old days, when the islands were less crowded and everything moved slower. Today, it was all about moving bodies from place to place without disturbing the real Hawaii. Of course, all of the tourist bodies translated into money, and the money provided a happier paradise. Wesley's happiness was derived from not having to deal with any of it. His idyllic life was a blessing, an inheritance that could last several lifetimes, bequeathed from his father Chan, whom he still missed and thought of every day. Meanwhile, he was rich and reveled in the freedom it gave him.

He slipped through the crowds with an eye out for blue uniforms. Wesley was sure that it was just a matter of time before the HPD tracked him down and booked him into the pokey…thanks to Bribaby. He worshipped Briar, but trouble just seemed to follow her everywhere she went. Auntie Cyd was the same; he was convinced they were cut from the same cloth and always marveled at their chutzpah. He was just the opposite. Wesley thought of himself as a shrewd old west poker player, who kept his hand close to the vest, and never counted anything in front of others. A man of constant awareness—that was him. He knew also that he was kind, obedient, brave, trustworthy…blah, blah, blah—and far less of a daredevil than either of his female relatives.

His heart skipped a beat as a uniformed cop bumped into him coming out of a men's room.

"Ohh, ah, ah," he stuttered nervously.

"Are you okay, Sir?" the uniform said, as he grabbed Wesley by the elbows.

"Uh huh…yes—it's just that you startled me. I'm okay; I swear I am." Wesley was sweating profusely.

“Sorry, *brah*, I didn’t mean to scare you. Here, take a sip of water, you’ll feel better.” The cop pulled him over to the bubbler between the Men’s and Ladies’ rooms.

Wesley—afraid not to comply, shuffled along with the cop. He had an urgent need to pee, but held it back. He bent as the officer pushed the on button. Wesley let the cool water fill his mouth and straightened up.

“Say, wait a minute. Don’t I know you?” the cop asked, leaning in close to Wesley’s face.

“I don’t think so…I mean, I’m, I’m nobody that you would know…Officer.”

The pee-urge returned, his knees involuntarily locked together, and he bent forward.

“Are you sure you’re okay?” the cop asked, placing a hand on Wesley’s shoulder.

“I just really have to go pee, Officer.”

“Hell, man, then go. Don’t do it out here with all these tourists around,” he laughed.

Wesley made for the men's room and bellied up to an open urinal just in time. "Woo-boy, close call."

As Wesley stepped back and zipped up, the cop was standing nearby, waving a finger knowingly.

"I got it now; you're that guy on television, *Dancing with the Stars*. Am I right, am I right?" he said, pleased with himself.

"Uh, no, Sir. I told you, I'm no one…honest."

"No way, I never forget a face." He reached for his notepad as he spoke. "How about an autograph for my girl."

Wesley took the pad and pen, ready to vomit from fear. Thinking the cop must have him confused with Ricky Martin, he quickly scribbled on the pad and handed it back.

"*Karl Marx*! You got to be kidding me. Is that your real name?"

“Yes, Sir, it is. My father was a redneck and thought it would be funny to name his son Karl. It was that or Elvis.” He shrugged.

“Poor bastard. Must be hell to be named after a commie pinko,” the cop commiserated.

“It is hell, Sir. Am I free to go?”

“Sure, sure, go ahead. What, you think I was going to throw you in the tank just because you got a commie name? Get outta here before I change my mind,” he laughed and nudged Wesley to the door.

Wesley headed straight for the nearest terminal bar.

“What’ll it be, buddy?”

“Make it an Old Fashioned—and make it quick.”

Wesley spotted Briar making her way past the security point into the terminal proper. He was always struck by her beauty and poise. When they were kids, she tried to teach him how to pose, rather than just sit or stand. For her, it was a natural fluid motion from one angled pose to another; for him, it was like stubbing a toe. For years, they had both tried to copy Auntie Cyd's famous "walk"—a subtle pivoting of her feet with each step. It was both mesmerizing and perplexing for all who watched. It really required high heels to perfect it, however, which was a commitment Wesley wasn't willing to make.

"Briar, over here," he waved his hand over his head to catch her attention.

"God, am I glad to see you," she said, as she looked around.

"Well, I can't say the same. You don't know what I've been through getting here. If you didn't show in another five minutes, I was leaving. This is not a safe place for me, thanks to you."

"Are you still obsessing over the speeding and parking thing? Let it go, Wesley. We have bigger things to be worried about."

"What's more important than my freedom, Bri? Look at me, do you have any idea what would happen to this gorgeous hunk of man inside a cage with a bunch of sex-starved beasts? My obit would read, 'Died from boarding,' and I'm not talking water boarding. Do you know the survival rate in prison for handsome guys like me?"

"Oh, you little drama queen, with emphasis on the 'queen'! You're always looking at worst case scenarios. I'm the one in trouble," she said anxiously, looking around again.

Unconsciously, they slipped their sunglasses on simultaneously, same gesture, same mannerism. Satisfied that their first line of defense was up, they left the alcove bar and made for the exit.

Chapter 8

The penthouse smelled the same as Briar remembered…a mixture of Auntie's favorite perfumes, fresh exotic flowers, and an underlying smell of something else…paradise, she supposed. It's how heaven must smell, Briar thought to herself. The apartment was spotless, a trait learned early and carried forward by both Wesley and Briar. The view from the wrap-around floor to ceiling stackable glass doors was beyond breathtaking. Diamond Head was off to the east, pristine ocean to the south, and the beaches of Waikiki to the west.

"Who's in there?" Wesley called out, as he and Briar entered the penthouse, hearing groaning sounds coming from the bedroom wing of the apartment.

"It's just me, Wesley. Don't come in here—I don't want you to see me this way." The voice was muffled, but Wesley and Briar both recognized it as Porter's. They rushed toward the sound, finding him on his bedroom floor, crying and doubled over in pain.

"Porter, what happened to you?" Wesley wailed.

Together, they gently lifted him from his knees and helped him over to the bed. The poor man's body was a patchwork of deep blue bruises, the side of his face was swollen out of shape, and his lips were puffed and ringed with dried blood. Both eyes were blood-tinged and wet with tears.

"Porter, Porter, stop crying and tell us what happened," Briar demanded.

Wesley ran to the bathroom and hurried back with a wet hand towel and a first aid kit.

"Let me see that face; stay still, I know it hurts," he cooed, as he gently dabbed at the wounds.

"We need to call the paramedics; he needs medical attention…like now." Briar pulled her iPhone from her hip pocket to make the call.

“No! Don’t call. He’ll kill me. He said he would kill me if I told anyone…” Porter lisped through broken teeth.

“Who?” Wesley demanded. “Who said they would kill you? Damn it, Porter, it looks like he already tried.”

“Porter, I think your jaw is broken, and those bites on your back need attention before they become infected,” Briar said, as she hit the 911-speed dial button.

“Wesley, I think he may have damaged me badly…inside,” Porter said, lowering his eyes. “The bleeding…it won’t stop.” Wesley suddenly noticed the blood seeping out from under Porter, creating a widening stain on the bedspread. Briar quickly returned with towels to place underneath him until help arrived.

“That’s it. Give me his name. He’s dead! I’ll kill the bastard…” Wesley stood, shaking with rage as he started out of the bedroom.

"Where are you going? Get back in here," Briar called out. "I've got to go downstairs and let the paramedics in."

"I'm getting my pistol. Porter's going to give me that beast's name, and I'm going to kill him. That's where I'm going. No one fucks with me or mine."

"Calm down, Wesley," Briar demanded. "When did you get to be such a badass? This isn't the time for you to go all bat-shit crazy on me. We need to take care of Porter first…payback can come later."

Three hours later, the ER unit doors opened and the surgeon appeared in the hospital waiting room, clipboard in hand.

"How is he, Doctor?" Wesley asked, as he rushed forward with Briar close behind.

"Your dad's a lucky man, Mr. Barrett. (Wesley looked at Briar and rolled his eyes, but didn't bother to correct the doctor). He is in ICU now; we'll keep him there overnight. He was brutalized pretty badly by whoever did this."

"But, he's going to be okay, right? He's not going to die, is he?" Wesley asked pleadingly.

"No, Mr. Barrett, but your father's not a young man. It is going to take him a long time to recover from the severity of these injuries."

"What do you mean, Doc?" Wesley asked, grabbing the doctor's arm. "By the way, Porter is not my dad; he's my lover."

The doctor looked at Briar, then back to Wesley, and said, "He had quite a bit of damage done to his colon; something was used to puncture the walls, and then…rotated. That is the only way I can describe it. We had to remove the colon, and quite a bit of the intestine. One procedure because of the irreparable damage, the other to keep the area from becoming infected."

"What are you saying? You mean Porter doesn't have a colon now? I'm not sure I completely understand what you're telling me."

“Take it easy, Mr. Barrett. He’s going to be all right. There are adjustments that he will need to make, and become accustomed to…but, the most important thing is that he’s alive.”

“He’ll have to live with a colostomy bag, is that it, Doctor?” Briar said.

“Exactly, Miss. The bite marks, the broken jaw, the cuts and contusions will heal with no lasting damage. The colostomy may be difficult to for him to adjust to physically. Psychologically, it could also be challenging for a while.”

Briar and Wesley exchanged looks. She saw something different in his eyes, something she had never seen before, something almost primal. She made a quick mental note to hide Wesley’s guns until all this was behind them.

“You know, of course, that these types of cases must be reported to the police. They need to know that something like this occurred.”

“Doctor, Porter was very worried about revealing the name of the person that did this to him. He said the person would kill him if he told. Can't you just delay that report until I've had a chance to resolve this myself?" Wesley said.

"I'm sorry, Mr. Barrett, but it's for just that reason that I must report it, and hopefully get this person off the streets before he can do any more harm. As for you resolving the issue yourself, I would strongly recommend you stay as far away as possible from anyone capable of doing something this gruesome to another human. He is obviously not a sane person, and you could end up being his next victim. Better let the authorities handle this, son."

Chapter 9

Briar left Wesley sitting outside the intensive care unit, with instructions for him to call her immediately if there was any change to Porter's condition. It was after 9 p.m., she had a mild case of jetlag, and she was hungry, exhausted, and in need of some "alone time" to clear her head and organize her thoughts. A good soak in a hot bubble bath and a solid eight hours sleep in Auntie's comfortable bed with cool, fresh linen would work wonders to revive her, both mentally and physically.

The late night air was clean and crisp, blowing her red hair wildly as she sped *ewa* toward Diamond Head on H-1 (Honolulu's main freeway). She turned the radio on and punched a few buttons until she heard Adele belting out "Rolling in the Deep." She tapped her hands rhythmically on the steering wheel to the beat as she took the Vette up to a hundred. The tachometer sat at 4500 rpm's; Briar exhaled. She knew that with a little goose to the gas, the powerful engine would jump to six thousand rpm's, and over a hundred and thirty mph.

The music, the speed, and the fresh air all filled her with a feeling of power, of omnipotence, of invincibility. The fear of being a suspect in Craig Stanton's murder slipped away; she was innocent and she was going to prove it. She felt an unbelievable release of guilt and culpability as her resolve hardened. Her fatigue melted away as she let up on the gas and allowed the speed to fall down under the speed limit. The last thing she needed was to be stopped by a traffic cop. She had so many tickets now that she'd probably couldn't sweet talk her way out of getting another. Especially if it was a female cop, like the last three times. Gosh darn it—policewomen just weren't as easily swayed by her devastating good looks, Briar chuckled to herself.

She steered the yellow Corvette carefully into Zippy's parking lot on Waialae Avenue, across from Kahala Mall. Already knowing what she wanted, Briar hopped onto a counter stool and ordered her favorite Belgian waffle, topped with vanilla ice cream, whipped cream, macadamia nuts, crushed pineapple, and Haupia sauce. She scarfed it down. She also picked up an order of sushi to leave in the fridge for Wesley, who'd be hungry when he dragged in later. He loved sushi at any time of day.

Poor little Wes, and good God—poor Porter! What could he have done to deserve the way he'd been abused? How could he (or they) get beyond this, and ever have their relationship be the same? She didn't understand exactly why, but she knew her cousin Wesley was very much in love with Porter. Now, he was totally consumed with wanting revenge in the worst way for what some psychopath did to his sweet old lover.

Briar left Zippy's feeling better and drove across the street into the deserted Kahala Mall parking lot. The popular mall was closed at this hour, with only a few parked cars scattered around the lot. Briar cut the engine and sat there for over an hour, gripping the steering wheel tightly as she pondered her next move. She was mentally arguing with herself about the plan that was formulating in her mind. What better place to start proving her innocence than with Craig's wife? Briar was a firm believer that one should go on the offensive when in danger. Craig's wife, Kalani, seemed like the perfect starting point. Kalani was the one who stood in front of the news cameras proclaiming, "*Find that woman, the Mainland whore, and you'll have your killer.*" Well, Briar wasn't a whore or the killer. Widow Stanton would need to be confronted and somehow convinced that Briar had not killed her husband. Sounded easy enough…

It was nearly midnight as Briar drove slowly down Black Point Road. The mansions on either side were dark; the occupants were fast asleep like sane folks at this hour. Or, the absentee owners had their homes shuttered tight against storms and break-ins. Briar knew that at least half of the homes in the ultra-rich Kahala neighborhood were owned by mainlanders or wealthy Japanese. They stood vacant for ten months out of the year with skeleton staff to maintain them. Then the owners would crash down on the Island for their annual parties, *luaus*, and society hobnobbing with the rich and famous. Then…just as quickly, they'd jet away to the next amusing venue.

She parked around the corner on Kaikoo Point. With her Coach Boho bag slung over her shoulder, she started walking toward Senator Stanton's home a half-block down. She and Ryan had spent a sin-filled afternoon here, while Kalani was away for the day on the Big Island. His home was situated on one of the choicest pieces of property in the area. Well, it actually was Kalani's property—passed down to her from generations of Popua ancestors. The Popua family was one of the richest families in the Islands, making their fortune from massive cane fields and sugar processing refineries. They were second only to Dole Foods for island exports. Senator Stanton was a poor *haole* mainlander when he first arrived in the Islands. Handsome, smart, and a social climber—he quickly set his sights on Kalani…primarily for her money, and secondarily for her beauty. He used her vast family connections to advance his career, and quickly became wealthy in his own right. Compared to Kalani's wealth, he was still a pauper, however—a fact she frequently reminded him of. The two realized early on that they were neither compatible in social situations or in marital bliss. Mostly because of his obstinate Boston Southey disposition, and his intense sexual appetite. On her side, she was a spoiled child raised with everything her family wealth could provide, along with her natural Hawaiian beauty. All of that contributed to the arrogance and snobbery.

Briar breathed the scent-laden darkness as she moved through the shadowy street. Tree frogs chirping off in the shrubbery fell silent at her passing. A lonely dog barked over towards Diamondhead, as night birds flitted overhead, hoary bats perhaps. Looking up and down the lane for any late night strollers or joggers, she walked quickly up the drive and onto the large entryway.

Putting her face up to the panel of glass that ran the height of the door, she saw that the foyer was dark except for a nightlight behind a large potted plant. Was Mrs. Stanton asleep? Briar tried the front door, but it was locked. She backed away from the door to consider her next move. She had come this far; she might as well go all the way.

Careful not to trip on the loose crushed-coral, she made her way around to the back of the house, across a large lanai, and over to the thatch-roofed pool house. A memory of the fun things she and Craig did inside the hut-like structure made her sad. She reached just inside the door and felt for the house key she knew would be there. People were so predictable, feeling secure in their casualness and routine, never realizing that anyone with above average common sense could break through the most difficult of security systems. Briar learned at the Academy that alarm systems were designed for one purpose and one purpose only—to alert someone that there has been a breach in their system. The key to successful B&E

was to disconnect the breaching system. In eighty percent of home security systems, the way to disconnect and reset the alarm is to hit the pound sign three quick times. She smiled at the proviso from the instructor, "If you hit the pound sign three times and the alarm still goes off, run like hell."

The key slid effortlessly into the lock on the side door leading into the garage. Briar held her small Maglite in one hand and a cylinder of pepper spray in the other, not sure what she would encounter. The last time she had been to the house there hadn't been any dogs, but you had to be prepared for any eventuality. The pungent smell of gasoline and oil filled the musty air. She ran a finger over the hood of a white Cadillac SUV, knowing it was dusty from the gritty trail left behind. Her light swept across a black Ford sedan and then onto a red Mercedes coupe, which she recognized as Craig's. All three cars were cold, and all three dusty.

"*Implying what, Briar?*" she said softly.

The door leading into the house creaked as she opened it. She stopped to listen, fearing that Mrs. Stanton would wake and come to investigate. She hit the pound key rapidly three times on the security system's pad.

"Predictably, security pads are usually just inside the garage door leading into the kitchen."

The house felt empty. It was hard to put her finger on why it felt empty—it just did. Rather than relaxing and dropping her guard, she became even more alert. She hated empty homes, especially ones that she had just broken into.

"Mrs. Stanton, are you home?" she said in a stage whisper.

No answer, no echo, no screams. The place was empty.

"Mrs. Stanton, yoo-hoo, it's the whore," she whispered sarcastically, not expecting an answer.

The place was empty, no one home. She let her hand holding the pepper spray fall to her side, and exhaled. She had been holding her breath without realizing it. Not really knowing what she was looking for, she began to shuffle through a basket on the kitchen counter, which was filled with opened mail, a note pad, a Chinese take-out menu, an open pack of Marlboro Lights, and packets of soy sauce…just odds and ends.

She entered the master bedroom cautiously, with her spray at the ready. No concealed carry permits were issued in Hawaii, and Briar felt naked without "Bob," her trusty Colt within easy reach. Meanwhile, pepper spray and martial arts were her island means of defense, until that state law was changed. Briar twitched her nose; the room smelled of sex. The bed was rumpled and unmade; a towel was draped over one side. She tiptoed to the bed and picked up the towel; it was damp. An ashtray on the night stand was filled with butts. Briar picked up a mangled butt…Marlboro Light. She opened the nightstand drawer and looked down on a chromed pearl-handled .45 automatic. She hefted the heavy pistol, not her size; she preferred her sweet 380—left in her apartment back in L.A. Craig mentioned having several pistols in the house, and this glitzy thing had to be one of them. Hawaii is a Castle Doctrine state, and has a stand-your-ground law. She started to put it back in the drawer, then changed her mind. Instead, she dropped it into her bag. It wouldn't hurt to have her own "stand your ground" piece—just in case. *"Just added another felony to my B&E."*

The bathroom smelled like gardenias and lavender, two smells particularly nauseating to Briar…but, obviously not to Kalani. She could still detect a slight odor of the Dolce Gabbana cologne Craig usually wore.

"Curiouser and curiouser."

The sound of a car pulling up the driveway sent a spasm of panic through her body. She hurried to the front entrance and peeked out the glass side-panel. Briar watched as the car stopped and the driver's door opened…then the passenger door. A portly man hurried around to help his passenger out—actually pulling, and not too gently either. Briar recognized Mrs. Stanton from photos she'd seen in issues of *Flux Hawaii* (a quarterly lifestyle magazine for the socially conscious), and also from the ostentatious portrait over the mantel in their living room. Briar had thought of her as Hawaiian royalty, or perhaps a modern day monarch. She was regal in the painting, but now she appeared to have had a few too many. Kalani hung onto her partner to keep from falling. Her partner was getting in a few gropes of his own, as he more or less carried her to the front door. Briar tore herself away from the spectacle and ran for the kitchen door. She slipped the door closed behind her, just as the kitchen lights came on. She stood, holding the doorknob tightly, and listening.

"Bobby, don't go, please." The words were slurred and barely coherent.

"I can't stay, my lovely. You know that I need to get home. We don't want to draw any attention to ourselves, now do we?"

"Oh, Bobby, I'm really despising you right now…and that 'tub of lard' you're married to." Kalani's voice was almost a whisper. "Just come to bed with me; I need you to hold me, tonight of all nights."

"I'll come by after the funeral tomorrow; I promise. It won't be long now and we can be together forever. Just be patient, my little bird."

As the voices grew fainter, Briar tiptoed out the side door and ran as fast as she could back in the direction of her car.

Chapter 10

Sergeant Kanoa and Sergeant Mano slid down in the unmarked car's front seat as Briar ran by. They had tailed the black sedan with Mrs. Stanton in the passenger seat from the Country Club, just out of curiosity more than with any purpose. They watched as Senator Craig's society wife left the Club, seeming to have had too much to drink, and acting too chummy with the mayor. *What's this all about*? It had been reported by the *Star-Advertiser*, that Mrs. Kalani Stanton was in seclusion, mourning her husband's death. Kimo's logical mind ran through the variables of such an occasion, seeing the mayor of Honolulu out drinking with the widow Stanton…but couldn't come up with a reasonable explanation.

Earlier, Kimo spotted his friend Detective Sergeant Eric Mano pull up in a plain-wrap unit, just as Kimo was exiting the coroner's building downtown. It was late afternoon, and he'd spent the last few hours reviewing the evidence in the Senator Stanton case. Kimo's mind was filled with speculation about the significance of a gecko inserted into the Senator's throat post-mortem. Geckos are everywhere in Hawaii—most homes and buildings have guardian geckos living within. They are considered good luck by locals. They are also excellent cockroach eliminators. Who wouldn't prefer a colorful little lizard in residence to a bunch of flying cockroaches? When Hawaiians say the hills are alive, they don't mean with the sound of music.

Mano called out to Kimo, "Howzit, *brah*? Wanna grind, den ride out Aina Haina? Gotta drop a file at the Chief's place." Eric Mano was a local boy—born and bred. He'd been an HPD cop longer than Kimo had. He'd never left the Islands, and never made an effort to curb his Pidgin English. He once told Kimo, "Mo bettah if da haole faka's not git me."

Kimo had no definite plans, other than to noodle over where to start his search for the killer. He was getting hungry and was anxious to *talk story* with his friend Mano. Maybe he would bounce some theories off him. Mano had keen instincts when it came to crime solving; he was much savvier than he liked to let on.

Kimo hopped into the black sedan, exchanging greetings, and clasping hands tightly.

"Ho, *bruddah*, try break my hand? I need dat one, she be my shootin' hand," Mano laughed.

"The only person you're going to shoot is yourself, *cuz*," Kimo laughed too, and squeezed harder.

After dropping off the folder at the Chief's house, they cruised through the Waialae Country Club's parking lot. They nosed into a space facing the large entrance, cut the motor, and fired up their cigarettes.

"How much you think it cost join dis club, *brah*?" Mano asked.

"Why even ask, *cuz*? You and me will never belong to dis place. Dis is old Hawaiian money…and new *haole* money."

"Japanese now too, Kimo." Mano dragged smoke deep into his lungs, then flipped the butt out the window in a shower of sparks.

"See dat, Kimo? See who jus' come out da club? Oh-ho, what is dis?"

They watched as the couple staggered arm in arm across the club's large portico, fumbling their way into a car parked in a reserved space.

"Follow them, Mano—let's make sure they get safely to their destination."

"You *lolo, brah*?" said Mano, shooting stink eye at Kimo. "You know who dat is?"

"Yeah, I know, it's the widow Stanton and Mayor Hilo. That's why we gotta follow 'em; something just don't feel right here."

Now, as they watched the red headed woman sprint past them—turn the corner and disappear, they bolted upright in their seats, staring quizzically at each other.

"Who da fak was dat?"

"I don't know, but let's tail her too," Kimo laughed.

The ignition ground weakly for a moment, finally kicking the motor over, using its last bit of juice. Mano exhaled and threw it in gear, making a tight U-turn. They made it to the corner, just as Briar (in the conspicuous yellow Corvette) pulled onto Black Point Road. The light late-night traffic on Kahala made it easy for Mano to keep the Vette in sight, but still lay back by a couple of blocks.

Briar spotted the dark sedan as she turned onto Elepaio Street; it was totally out of place for this side of Diamond Head—where BMWs, Mercedes, and Hummers were de rigueur. Anyone driving an old sedan around this area was either a thief or a cop. Briar decided they were cops and punched the Vette. She swung back around onto Diamond Head as the sedan fishtailed around the corner several blocks back. She kept her speed up as she blew past Kahala Mall and up the ramp onto H-1, back toward Waikiki.

There was no sign of the cop car as Briar drove down the ramp onto Kalakaua Avenue. A few minutes later, she was in the underground parking lot of Auntie's penthouse. She turned off the motor and sat for a minute, allowing her nerves to calm and her eyes to adjust to the garage's dim light. She was spooked by the day's events, feeling that one more shot of adrenaline to her system could put her over the edge.

Briar waited less than a minute for the elevator to arrive and take her up to the fifteenth floor and a soothing bath. The lobby was empty and quiet, and the Muzak system was off for the night. The elevator doors slid open soundlessly. She pressed the floor number and leaned against the cab wall—tired to the point of exhaustion. As she sped upward, Briar caught her reflection in the smoky-gray glass of the elevator interior and grimaced. The face looking back at her was drawn and tired. She ran a hand through her hair and sighed as the doors slid open on her floor.

Her heart stopped. The hallway was dark; the elevator cab's light cast a gloomy yellow swath across the tiled entry into the apartment. She could see only darkness beyond the open front door of her unit, like the maw of a faceless monster. She dug in her bag, feeling for the pistol she'd taken from Craig's nightstand.

Briar never took her eyes off that swath of light, thinking at any moment something would step into it, something she didn't want to see. Her hand searched around the clutter in her handbag, accidently snapping open the take-out container of Wesley's sushi. Bile climbed up her throat, fear becoming panic. Finally, as her fingers wrapped around the pistol's grip, she felt in charge again.

She held the heavy pistol in front of her as she stepped slowly out of the elevator and into total darkness. The elevator doors closed behind her as she crept silently down the hall.

Briar's hand snaked around the door casing, searching for the master switches that would light up the penthouse. She flicked them up, then down, up again, then down…no lights. She found her Maglite and ran the beam around the room. Everything seemed in place…so far, so good.

Briar whirled around at the sound of breaking glass. She squatted on one knee and aimed the pistol.

"Wesley, is that you? What's with the lights? It's me, Briar."

The quiet roared in her ears.

"Talk to me if you're in here, Wesley; I'm not messing around. If you don't speak up, I'll come in shooting."

At that moment, an enormous figure charged out of the bedroom, so unexpectedly that Briar dropped the Maglite, and before she could react or pull the trigger, the gun was kicked out of her hand. In the next instant, she was lifted and thrown across the room, slamming into a large Keane painting, mounted behind a plexi-glass case. The heavy case dislodged from the wall, landing squarely on Briar's head—knocking her out. She regained consciousness as she was being lifted again. This time, a smashing pain exploded in her face. By the dim moonlight streaming in through the windows, she could vaguely make out the profile of her attacker. Was she hallucinating, or was this big *moke* wearing glitter eye shadow? Her last thought before a zillion stars detonated across her mind…"Where's the gun? Where's that fucking gun?" She slumped to the floor, unconscious.

A kettledrum beat against her skull, pounding out a tattoo of torturing pain. She groaned at the ache shooting through her back and shoulder, where she had slammed against the wall. She remembered that part, and vaguely recalled being lifted, and then the lights went out. She rolled onto to her side, swiping gently at her eyes. The left eye was swollen shut, and the other felt caked with blood. She worked her jaw around with her hand; nothing was broken, thank God.

She carefully sat up, and then used a chair to steady herself as she stood. Peeking out of her right eye, she made her way into the kitchen and stuck her head under the faucet while turning it on. She filled her mouth with water, swished, and then spit the bloody mess out. The cold water did wonders for her headache and throbbing left eye. She wiped her face and head dry with a dishtowel, then took her first look around the apartment. Aunt Cyd was going to be pissed about the damage done to her priceless Margaret Keane painting, a gift from Uncle Duane during happier times.

Dawn light lit up the penthouse, bright enough that she could see her way around now to inspect the other rooms. In the living room, she searched for Craig's pistol, but it was gone. Her Coach bag had been emptied out on the floor. She checked her wallet, finding all of her credit cards and IDs were in their place.

“Glad he didn't take my driver license. I would take a black eye any day over having to deal with those idiots at the DMV in California again," she grumbled.

Briar followed a blood trail over to the closed front door and flipped the deadbolt. The man must have been somehow injured, she thought—then remembered hearing the sound of breaking glass before she was assaulted. She saw that the electrical fuse-box door was open. Disguised as decorative molding in a recessed alcove, the box was unnoticeable unless you were looking for it. The main panel switch was in the off-position. She gave it a lift and the apartment came to life with a whoosh of air, as the central air kicked in, along with a half dozen beeps from appliances demanding attention. She hurried into the kitchen, resetting the microwave, oven, toaster, and coffee maker. Automatically, she threw together a pot of Kona coffee…Briar liked it strong and in quantity.

With the coffee brewing, she headed toward Porter's room. The intruder had come from that direction, and it seemed the best place to start to find out what or who it was that broke in. Briar crinkled her nose at the powerful smell of cologne that hit her as she entered the room, “Whew, smells like a Turkish bathhouse,” Briar thought, amused by her analogy—never having been in a Turkish bath, or even knowing if Turks had bathhouses.

Porter’s large dresser had been tossed, and the contents were strewn around the room. The many bottles of expensive cologne had been swept off the dresser top and were broken and draining onto the tile floor. The man was looking for something; he wasn't here to steal. Briar knew instinctively that this was the same psycho who had taken bites out of Porter’s back as he was probably raping him. Briar didn't bother going into the large walk-in closet; all of the clothing had been ripped from the hangers, turned inside out, and covered the closet floor.

The bathroom walls were covered in splashes of blood. The shower door had been shattered, the toilet's porcelain tank cover had been smashed to pieces, the sink was cracked, and the medicine cabinet door was torn off its hinges. Blood was everywhere. Briar was shocked at the violent damage done. At some point, the search had turned into something more menacing, something more ominous. The intruder apparently had not found what he was looking for, and the violence provoked more violence…to the point of the person becoming murderously enraged. She realized at that moment how lucky she was to be alive.

She stood, trying to make sense of it all, when her eyes fixated on something drawn in blood on the wall above the tub. She didn't recognize what she was seeing at first. Once she realized just what it was, her brow wrinkled in puzzlement.

"A gecko?"

Chapter 11

With a cup of steaming hot coffee in one hand, holding an ice pack to her eye with the other, her phone lay on the counter in front of her, as Briar hit Wesley's speed dial number, setting it on speaker. Waiting for him to pick up, she grabbed the remote, turning on the small flat screen television mounted on the wall above the breakfast bar. Like the TVs in every other room, it was tuned to KOHN2, Honolulu.

"Hello Briar…Briar…BRIAR, are you there?" Wesley boomed.

Briar was preoccupied, watching the news about Craig Stanton's funeral scheduled for 1:00 that afternoon.

"Hold just a minute," Briar said.

"…The delegation of senior senators from Washington will touch down at HNL around noon, proceeding directly to Punchbowl National Cemetery, where the graveside services will be held…"

Briar lowered her face to the phone and asked, "Angel, are you okay…is everything okay with Porter?"

"I'm okay—just exhausted from a restless night of trying to sleep in a chair next to Porter's bed. What's going on with you? You don't sound good, Bri. Are you getting a cold?"

"Listen Wesley, you are not going to believe what all happened after I left the hospital last night. I'll give you details when I see you, but I've been on the ground less than twenty-four hours, and have committed a break and entry, burgled a senator's home, witnessed a grope session between the drunk widow and some fat slob, had the cops chase me all around Diamond Head, got beat-up and nearly killed in my own apartment, and to top it off—there is a gecko painted IN BLOOD on Porter's bathroom wall. Other than that, just another beautiful day in Paradise," Briar quipped.

"Whoa, whoa, WHOA, Briar, what the hell are you talking about? You texted me at 9:15 last night that you were eating ice cream, and going home to bed. Where did you go after that? What do you mean you were almost killed? A bloody gecko—what the fuck???"

"First, tell me if you have seen a large *moke*, possibly wearing glitter eye shadow, hanging around the ICU area?"

"Briar, take a Xanax and go back to bed. You're spinning out of control, girl."

"*I'm not spinning out of control, dammit!*" Briar forced herself to regain control. She caught her reflection in the toaster, noticing she'd developed a pair of shiners. She took a deep breath and continued calmly. "I'm asking you specific questions, Wesley, which require simple yes or no answers. So, let's start over, shall we?" Briar struck a pose of rationality—eyes cast upward, chin on fist.

"Okay, you have my attention, Bri," Wesley said, "Now, what was that about some *mahu* in eye shadow?"

"You're alive, so I'll safely assume he hasn't been there yet," she said tightly. "I can tell you firsthand, Wesley—you don't want to meet up with this psycho. The only calling card he left here (other than a bruised and mangled 'me'), was a bloody bathroom and a crude drawing of a gecko above Porter's bathtub."

"He was there? In the Penthouse?" Wesley demanded, suddenly frantic at the thought that Porter's rapist had been inside their home. "Do you need medical attention, Briar? Why didn't you call the police? Do you think it's even safe for you to be there alone? Is anything missing?"

"I don't know—I don't know anything for sure right now," Briar sighed. "I think he got Craig's chromed pearl-handled .45 automatic that I lifted last night from his nightstand. I was holding it when I entered the apartment, and now I can't find it anywhere, but never mind…I'll fill you in on everything when I come to the hospital after Craig's funeral. Right now, I need to go find something somber to wear."

"Bri, should even go to that funeral? I'm sure the grieving widow will be less than thrilled to see you there. She knows what you look like from the pics on the flash drive, and it's not like you are inconspicuous, with that mop of copper hair. What about wearing a wig, or at least tucking it up under a hat or something?" Wesley advised.

"I don't want to go, but I have to be there, Wes! Out of respect for Craig (a man I sort of loved), but mainly because somewhere in that gathering could be Craig's killer. If I can make eye contact with whoever it is, I'll know immediately if they are the murderer. Although, it may be difficult for me to make eye-contact with anyone from behind the huge sunglasses I'll be wearing to conceal these ugly shiners. Before I forget, how's Porter's condition?" Briar asked.

“Not good, he’s running a high fever and is getting dehydrated, in spite of all the fluids they are pumping into him. The doctor will be making his rounds soon, and I’ll know more after that.”

“Okay, just stay with Porter. I’ll come there straight from the funeral. We’ll talk, and after that you can go home and get some rest.”

The flashback of last nights’ terrifying encounter, then later cleaning up the blood and broken glass in Porter’s bathroom, gave her chicken skin. Goosebumps were running a marathon up her arms and down her back as she made a lame attempt at cleaning up. She took pictures with her phone of everything, including the bloody gecko, to show Wesley. Before running her bath, she propped a dining room chair under the front doorknob. If anyone tried to get in, she would at least hear them coming, having enough time to snatch up the 9mm Ruger she took from Wesley’s sock drawer. She glanced over at the pistol sitting on the toilet lid and attempted to smile. “Ouch—that hurts.”

Calling the police about the break-in was out of the question. Once she identified herself, she would be cuffed and hauled downtown—imagining the old gumshoe jargon reminded her of the instructors at the Academy and brought another painful smile to her swollen face. Wesley was right—if one Xanax is good, then two will be primo.

She popped the pills, switched on the tub's relaxing air jets, closed her eyes, and let herself drift. She needed sleep, just a few minutes is all…

She spluttered awake, spitting soapy water, grabbing the tub sides, and pulling herself up out of the deep tub into a sitting position. Perching on the side of the tub, Briar grabbed a spa-sized towel and patted herself dry. Dropping the towel and walking naked into Auntie's huge closet, she found a simple Armani sleeveless shift dress—perfectly suitable for the day. She spotted an Eric Javits black straw sun hat on a top shelf, which would complement the dress and hide most of her hair…thus, perhaps, not calling too much attention at the cemetery. In twenty minutes, she was ready and standing in front of the full-length mirror, approving her look, except for the swollen black eyes. Wesley's Prada shades, that she'd spied earlier on his dresser would cover most of that. Her favorite Phillip Lim black triangle handbag had a secret compartment, into which she could secure the Ruger. *No conceal carry—no problem.* After last night, she wasn't taking any chances.

Her hand resting on the doorknob, Briar paused to take a deep breath before heading out. As the elevator closed and she pressed the button for the parking garage—she couldn't help wondering, "*What kind of trouble might she encounter today*?"

Chapter 12

The senate chaplain had just quoted the Blessing of the Virgin Mother at Lourdes from his personal prayer book—a gift from Pope Paul. He then launched into a lengthy homily of Senator Stanton's good works for the Islands, and most especially for the indigenous peoples of Hawaii.

Briar stood in the back of the large crowd. Even with the sunglasses and the wide-brimmed hat, she worried that if she pushed forward, she would draw attention to herself. Instead, she slowly worked her way around the back edge of the crowd, looking closely at each person. So far, she hadn't recognized anyone except Mrs. Stanton sitting graveside under the awning. Kalani Stanton rocked back and forth, sobbing loudly and reaching dramatically for the casket with outstretched arms with each piercing wail. Two Hawaiian women sat on either side of Kalani, sobbing and chanting an old Hawaiian prayer. The good Father shot cutting glances at the women, with each calling out to the god and goddess

Wãkea and Pele, so loved and respected by the Hawaiian people. The old Franciscan priest knew devil worship when he saw it, and he didn't appreciate the competition either.

The half-circle of notables and visitors gathered around the casket and under the awning—for the bereaved numbered in the hundreds. Briar stood out in the crowd like a bright red ginger flower; even with what she thought was a subdued outfit. She noticed the stares she was getting, from both men and women.

She spotted the cop keeping pace with her by his wrinkled suit and sophomoric effort to tail her. She would stop, and he would stop and gaze at the sky. It became a game, and after the third stop-and-go, she turned and strode up to him purposefully, coming nose to nose.

"You little prick. If you keep following me, I'm calling a cop—now scram."

Kimo, not accustomed to gorgeous women talking to him, was so flustered that he could only stutter.

"No…no, Ma'am, I'm not following you. Well, I am—but not like that…"

"So, you are stalking me; you admit it," Briar demanded, enjoying the man's discomfort. "That settles it; I'm calling a cop."

Briar fumbled for her phone in her bag, not taking her eyes off the man.

"No need to call the cops, Ma'am…I…I'm the cops. I mean, I am a cop," he blurted out, as he flipped his jacket open to expose the badge on his belt. "I didn't mean to alarm you, Miss Malone."

Briar's blood chilled to daiquiri level, at hearing her name.

"How do you know my name?" she stage whispered, as several mourners shot them *stink eye*.

"I can explain it to you," he said, as he touched her elbow lightly, guiding her away from the crowd.

Once they were several yards away, Kimo turned and raised his hands in surrender.

"Hear me out, Miss Malone. I know who you are, and that some in Honolulu think you are connected to Senator Stanton's murder. I'm not one of them. I know you were his lover, but then you returned to Los Angeles well before the Senator was killed. How could you have killed him from two thousand miles away? And what would be your motive…compromising photos taken in Suite 222 at the Royal Hawaiian Hotel? Why would you be worried about any compromise to your reputation—you aren't married, and you have nothing of value other than your lost shipment of house wares…"

"Hold it right there, Dano! How is it that you know so much about me and what do you know about my lost shipment? Who the hell are you, anyway?"

Kimo shuffled his feet humbly, and said, "I'm just a local cop trying to piece some clues together, Miss Malone. My name is Kimo Kanoa; I am a homicide detective with the HPD. I have access to the same database that you used during the brief time you were with the FBI. It was easy finding out who you are and what your relationship with the senator was."

"Oh, really, so it was simple for you to find out my name, and where I live, and where I went with the senator?"

"Yes, Ma'am," Kimo said smiling. "I recognized the executive suite at the Royal Hawaiian from the photographs; the rest was easy…"

"You saw the photos on my personal flash drive?!" Briar thumped Kimo's chest with a finger, "You have no business looking at those pictures; they are private and…and confidential. You perverted bastard!" Briar punched Kimo's chest with each syllable. "I want that flash drive back, and all the copies you creeps made…otherwise, I'll sue your ass, the police chief and…and the frigging governor too…"

She stomped her foot and swung her head to the side in anger. Just the thought of her naked images in the hands of strangers humiliated her. She wanted to kick something…or someone.

"Miss Malone, pardon me, but you must calm down; there are people at the funeral who would love to apprehend you. Please, calm down."

Briar knew the cop was right; she needed to cool her jets. Maybe this imbecilic moron could help her clear her name.

"Look, Dano, if you know so much about me, then you know that I am probably the number one suspect, so why aren't you cuffing me?"

"I'm not after you, Miss Malone. I'm after the man who killed the senator. But I do have a question for you. Where were you last night around 2300, uh, sorry, around eleven?"

"Home in bed, Dano, where all good girls should be that late at night. What's your point?"

"Hmmm, I wonder how many Vintage yellow Corvettes there are in Honolulu and how many would be cruising around Kahala at that hour?" Kimo turned in the direction of the bright yellow car parked among the dozens of black government vehicles on the narrow cemetery lane.

Briar cut her eyes toward the Vette, and without hesitation she grabbed his jacket roughly and pulled him to her.

"So, you're the prick that tried to chase me down last night. What was that all about? You could have gotten us killed."

Kimo grabbed Briar's wrists and squeezed; she was surprised at the strength of Kimo's hands, and saw that his knuckles were hardened by hours of karate.

"Miss Malone, cut the crap. You and I both know that you were at the senator's home last night. Something spooked you, and you ran back to your car. You were within five feet of me and my partner. I recognized you immediately by the red hair," he said through gritted teeth. "Now, knock off the *Hawaii Five-O* sarcasm, and listen up."

Kimo released her wrists, patted her hands, and said, "I'm sorry, Miss Malone, if I hurt you, but you need to listen to me. There are two very important things you need to know if you want to clear yourself of any suspicion in the senator's murder. The first is that the murder was undoubtedly planned and arranged by someone right here at the funeral," as he nodded his head back to the graveside crowd.

"It could be any one of those people. His wife is a strong possibility, although I'm not sure what her motive would be. Or, it could be Jimmy Hinoko, his opponent in the senatorial race. Elected officials can steal millions of dollars with a stroke of a pen in Washington, but Jimmy already has more money than he could ever spend. Maybe it was one of his senate colleagues. Look at them checking their watches every few seconds; they don't want to be here. They're off the clock, and time is money to each of them." Kimo took Briar by the elbow and guided her farther away from the crowd.

"So, Miss Malone, here are the known's and unknowns that we must sort through. Who arranged for the murder? What was the motive? Money? I don't think so. Perhaps political power. Was it just a random killing and we are wasting our time trying to read something more into his death than what really happened?"

"Why did you say *we* must sort through the knowns and unknowns, Detective?" Briar asked suspiciously. "Last time I watched the six o'clock news, *I* was suspect number one."

"Your accusers said that you are a suspect, and the media just ran with it. The last time *I* checked, you were not a suspect."

"Maybe you need to check higher up the cop chain, Detective. Sometimes it takes a while for word to filter down to the street cops."

Kimo's toothy grin lit up his face. "In this case, you are the lucky one. I am the higher-up that decides who the suspects are, and you are not one."

"Oops, sorry. I didn't mean to be rude or insulting," Briar said, pulling back from her defensive mode, actually beginning to like this unassuming man. He was even kind of cute…all that beautiful black hair and those chubby cheeks looked so pinch-able. "You don't have any idea how relieved I am at hearing that you guys don't have an A.P.B. out on me. I've been ducking around corners and looking over my shoulder since I arrived yesterday."

"As you should continue to do, Miss Malone. We are dealing with a deranged individual, who is spinning out of control. With each new kill, he is becoming more aggressive and more violent. He's seemingly unafraid of being caught."

"I don't understand. What are you talking about? Aren't we trying to find the person that killed Craig Stanton?" Briar said, confused.

"Yes, we are talking about the same thing. That's why I need your help. I'm asking you to use your FBI investigative training to determine who the mastermind is behind the murder, while I find the actual killer."

"I still don't understand. You think the murder was planned by one person, and carried out by another?"

"Yes, I do. Look over at the crowd. Do you see anyone that might have the strength to break a man's neck, rape him, carry him up a steep slippery hill in the dark, and then throw him over a waist-high barrier into a raging waterfall?"

Briar swooned for a moment, quickly catching her balance before Kimo spotted her. Her mind whirled in confusion at what had happened to Porter, the massive damage to his colon, and the bite marks on his back. The thought of Craig having had the same thing done to him blew everything else out her mind. She needed to call Wesley and somehow get them both the hell out of that hospital before the killer came back for them.

"Are you all right, Miss Malone? You look pale as *poi*."

I…I'm fine. It's the heat. I've been away from the Islands for a while, and I'm not used to the sudden climate change…"

Kimo looked closely at her, not believing for a second that the heat was getting to her. He had seen her stagger at the mention of how Craig had been murdered.

"I'm sorry, Miss Malone; I didn't mean to upset you with the details. I just assumed, being an FBI agent, you would want to know the circumstances of his death."

"Yes, yes, of course. If I'm going to help you, I'll need all the facts about the actual murder," she said, regaining her composure. "Tell me, Kimo…may I call you Kimo?"

"Only if I can call you Briar."

"Of course you can. Kimo, were there any other marks or damage to the body that I should know about?"

Kimo's radar was on full alert at her question. She knew something, but what? Should he tell her about the bites on Stanton's back and the same bite patterns on the backs of the three other murder victims?

"No, just cuts, bruises, and broken bones from tumbling down the waterfall," he lied. He made it a point to not mention the gecko either. He would keep that particular tidbit of information to himself for now.

Briar (with radar of her own) knew he had just lied to her. She was petrified at the thought that the person who killed Craig had somehow been the same person that almost killed Porter. And possibly was the same big *moke* who knocked her around in the apartment the night before. She was taught to question coincidences, because there were rarely such things as coincidences in murder cases. The threat made by the perp to Porter, that he would be killed if he reported the brutal rape and beating to the police, flashed across her mind in bright neon lights. She also needed to know more about what Kimo knew about the killer, and who he thought was behind the murder.

"Kimo, you said that the M.O. in Craig's case is the same as three other cases? Tell me about the others, maybe with both of us on the same wavelength, we can stop this guy from doing it again."

“His murders fit the classic pattern of a serial killer. He is a loner, possibly has a history of cruelty to other children when he was young. Probably a bully, maybe liked to hurt or kill small animals, loved his father, hated his mother…all the basics.”

Briar recalled her instructor at Quantico saying that “*Your mainstream serial killer would rather chop up his mother into stew meat than play outside with other kids after school.*” The overriding thrill with a serial killer is the powerful life and death dominance he holds over his victims as he is killing them. Each killing becomes more violent than the one before—often with something taken from the victim as a trophy, or a talisman left behind to taunt the authorities. The serial killer becomes less cautious with each new killing; rationality disappears and he becomes less restrained, letting himself go completely, until the only way he can be stopped is by being killed or caught. However, until either of those two things happen, he will continue to kill.

"This is scaring me, Detective."

"We don't know that he's not working alone, Briar," said Kimo. "Maybe Stanton just happened to be in the wrong place at the wrong time."

"No, I'm not buying it. Why would the killer take the trouble to put the flash drive into Craig's shoe if he hadn't been told to? Remember—the flash drive was used as a way of drawing attention away from someone, and on to someone else. Me, for example," Briar said.

"You're very clever, Miss Malone. That's the same assumption that my department head, Captain Ping Lee, would like for me to make. It may be a correct assumption, but my objective is to find the mongoose first, then the snake. So, have we agreed that two heads are better than one? Especially when one of the heads is a trained FBI investigator?"

"Kimo, if you really did check my background, then you would know that I was kicked out of the Agency for being a troublemaker. So, stop with all the bonhomie hail good fellow crap, and tell me more about the serial killer."

"I can tell you what I know and what I think, but I can't tell you who he is," he said. "The other three murders all happened in the Waikiki and Kahala areas. One of the three was a tourist from Nebraska staying at the Sheraton on the beach, another was a Navy commander stationed at Pearl, and the third was a male stripper at a club on South Hotel Street. The murders were exact in every case, except each was more violent than the previous. Senator Stanton's was identical, except for the location and the severity of his injuries. My guess is that Stanton was murdered in the same area as the others, and then taken to Sacred Falls to be found. Why the change to the pattern? I don't know."

"My instinct tells me his wife, Kalani, is behind it," Briar said. "Somehow, she got her hands on the flash drive with the photos and flipped out when she saw what her hubby was doing behind her back. Jealousy is a very strong motivator; more than one philandering hubby has gotten whacked from straying away from home."

"Yes, but how would a woman of her stature in the community know how to arrange a murder with an insane serial killer? Where is the connection between her and the killer?" Kimo wondered.

"Good point, Kimo. However, her family is large and scattered around the Islands, in every city and town. Maybe there's some cousin or uncle that could have connected her up with him."

Briar and Kimo both swung their heads toward the sound of crashing and screaming coming from the ceremony.

Kalani Stanton was crying and screaming, as two of her "attendants" beat Jimmy Hinoko and his wife with their parasols. Briar and Kimo hurried closer to see what it was all about.

"You murderer! You killed my husband," Kalani was screaming, slapping Jimmy as she yelled.

The chaplain tried to break up the fight, and was attacked by one of the attendants twice his size. He ducked several blows aimed at his head, and foolishly decided to fight back. He stood erect in his best boxing stance, and waited for an opening on the bulky target.

The attendant smiled, tossed her parasol to the side, and pushed up the sleeves on her calico patterned muumuu.

"Like beef? Shoots—come on den. Come to Leilani." She motioned for him to come closer, wiggling her fat fingers." You *pupuka 'okole*—dis *tita* gonna buss you up."

The good Father saw his opening, advanced forward (as he was taught at the Point), leading with an uppercut to her huge jaw. In the next second, he was on his back, knocked unconscious by "*da tita,*" and would remain so for the next several hours.

The ceremony collapsed into a small riot as the Hinoko clan and supporters mixed it up with Kalani's clan and Craig's supporters. It took the off-duty motorcade chaperones a half hour to separate the brawlers. Briar saw her opportunity to get away and warn Wesley about the trouble coming their way. She was worried sick as she goosed the Vette and roared down the narrow lane back out to H-1. She looked back over her shoulder in time to see Kimo signaling for his driver to pick him up.

Wesley answered his cell on the third ring, sounding exhausted.

"Get Porter up and ready to go; we've got trouble coming at us faster than Auntie can spot a rich sucker."

Chapter 13

It was late afternoon, and Briar's mind was red-lining as she sped *ewa* bound on H-1, toward downtown Honolulu and the hospital. The possibility of the serial killer being the same person that injured Porter was no coincidence. She needed to get Porter and Wesley out of that hospital and somewhere safe before the killer determined Porter to be too much of a risk to his freedom. Then there was the slugfest back at the cemetery—what was that all about? Kalani was crazy to confront Jimmy Hinoko like that; what was her game? The funeral ruckus could have been just a way to throw suspicion off of her and onto Jimmy. Why not, Jimmy had the most to gain by Craig's death, didn't he? The mainstream media could find him guilty with or without legitimate evidence proving otherwise. And, guess what wealthy family owned the Island's biggest and most influential newspaper and television station? Another guilt-point against Kalani fell into place in Briar's mind. If the MSN was going to convict

Jimmy, then the cemetery fight would be the lead story on the six o'clock news tonight.

Briar's phone chimed, pulling her back from her analysis. She did the one-handed scavenge through her bag for the phone, gave up, and just turned it upside down on the seat.

"Hello," she answered, without looking at caller I.D.

"Bribaby, it's Auntie Cyd. You didn't call, and I've been worried sick. I shouldn't have to chase you down. A simple call or text letting me know the plane didn't crash would have…"

"Auntie, slow down…slow down…Auntie…*Damn it, Cydny—slow down for one minute!!!"* Briar finally yelled into the phone.

After a moment's pause, Aunt Cyd spoke, "No need to be rude; I taught you better. A lady never needs to raise her voice; the right choice of words is far more effective than an impetuous voice. And…vulgarity is not necessary either."

"Yes, Auntie, but you kept going on and on. I'm in heavy traffic, and I can't concentrate on both you and my driving. Sorry—I guess I'm a little stressed at the moment."

"I take it that the apartment's not in a shambles? Wesley and his friend didn't sell everything of value and flee to Tahiti?" Auntie asked jokingly.

"Uh, no, it's not trashed…too much," she added, wincing.

"Too much? What does that mean?"

"Considering that two adult men are living there, I would have to say the place looks good. Other than for a few piles of stinky laundry and a sink full of dirty dishes, the apartment is fine, Auntie," she lied. Images of a shattered shower door, a cracked porcelain toilet and sink, drawers splintered, bloodstains on the carpet…all made her cringe with guilt.

And the painting! Oh, my God, that priceless "Big Eyes" portrait, painted by Margaret

Keane in the '70's of Auntie's beloved pets. Now that was a totally separate problem. The only way to resolve that loss was to contact Margaret Keane personally, tell her what happened, and beg her to repaint it. Even if she agreed, Briar's personal bank account couldn't handle it, and it would probably put a dent in Wesley's inheritance too. Otherwise, they'd both better prepare to commit the ancient samurai tradition of *seppuku*, as they begged forgiveness from Auntie.

"Well, that doesn't sound too bad. Thank God for small favors, right?"

"Yes, Ma'am, thank God for those."

"Now for the good news, I've decided to make Arturo an honest man and marry him. We have talked it over with each other and our attorneys, and have agreed it would be for the best. The poor dear is lonely and needs a wife. He has no family of his own, except for his mother. I feel I'm the right person to step into that breach, so to speak."

"Step into his money is more like it," Briar said under her breath.

"What was that?"

"Nothing, Auntie, so when is the big event?"

"That's the fun part, honey. We're doing it this weekend. And, are you ready? It will be on the beach at Waikiki. Surprise!" Peals of happy laughter came across the ether.

Briar froze, her eyes becoming pinpricks of anxiety. The cars in front of her were doing the vertigo boo-ga-loo. She shook her head to clear it.

"This weekend? On the beach at Waikiki? You and Arturo? Married? Holy crap!"

"Yes, dear, isn't that just the best news you've had all day? We'll arrive Friday evening on his company's Citation. A few friends will fly over with us, so I'll need for you to book rooms at the Royal Hawaiian. Oh, and before I forget, I'd like you to arrange a small dinner party at the apartment for twenty close friends. You know who to call. Keep it light on the food and heavy on the bubbly. This will be my sixth or seventh wedding—I forget exactly—but it will be my best. Aren't you excited for me, Bribaby?"

"Yes, very excited," she mumbled. Then, coming to her senses, "No, Auntie—you can't come to Hawaii! There's a…uh…a hurricane coming…tomorrow. It's forecasted to spin over the Islands for days…maybe even weeks…"

"What are you going on about? When did a hurricane ever stop a party of mine in the islands—much less a wedding? We'll just move it inside if need be. Now, be a darling, and call a caterer. Isn't Wesley's friend Porter some kind of caterer? Talk to him about it, why don't you?"

"Yeah…well, that's obviously not gonna happen," said Briar quietly under her breath, as she ended the monkey-wrench of a call from Aunt Cyd.

Her head was still spinning with instructions from Aunt Cyd as she pulled into the hospital's patient parking lot. She was tired from lack of sleep and her nerves were stretched so tight she could play them like harp strings—only she imagined that the sound would be similar to a cat in heat. Detective Kanoa's warning that the serial killer was at his "snapping-point," and would probably kill again soon, made her even edgier. Porter's assailant had to be the same guy; the similarities were beyond coincidence.

Wesley had nodded off in a guest chair he'd commandeered from the waiting room, and was snoring lightly. The poor guy was a rumpled mess with dark circles beneath his beautiful brown eyes. Briar's deep affection for him made her heart beat faster in her chest. She loved him more than anyone else in the world, and felt sick at the thought of the terrible trouble they were in. They had been through a lot together over the years, but this was on a much different level. This was trouble of the life-changing…if not life-ending variety.

Her first inclination was to wake him and together tiptoe out of the room—away from Porter's trouble…never looking back. She knew Wesley would never do that. He was too loyal and protective of Porter to just leave him alone to face what was coming. Wesley would never abandon anyone—he had always had great loyalty and integrity, even as a small boy.

Briar flashed back to an incident that occurred shortly after her adoption by the Malone's. Mike Malone also had another son (Brandon) from a previous marriage. Brandon was a troubled fifteen year-old boy (five years older than Wesley and Briar). He lived in St. Louis with Mike's ex-wife, who was still single. Brandon got suspended from school for fighting, so his mom sent him to spend the summer with his Dad, hoping Mike could straighten the kid out. Wesley and Briar felt uneasy around Brandon, so they left him to interact with his dad and Uncle Chan in the garage, making last minute mechanical adjustments to their drag boats before loading them onto the trailers. It was a Friday night, and the family would leave early the next morning for Table Rock Lake, where Uncle Chandler was racing in a national competition. Briar's two older step-brothers and Wesley's brother, Adam, were all away at Scout camp, so Wesley decided to sleep in the boys' room upstairs next to Briar's bedroom. Brandon was to sleep in the den downstairs. It was nearly midnight when Briar awoke to see someone sitting on the edge of her bed, smoking a smelly joint. She knew what pot smelled like, from living with her mom. As moonlight streamed in through her bedroom window, she had no problem recognizing Brandon. She raised herself up on her elbows to speak, as Brandon turned and held the joint toward her saying, "Here, take a drag, Briar." Although some kids at the orphanage smoked cigarettes, and a few of the older kids smoked weed too (when they could get it), Briar was never interested in smoking anything. She'd been exposed to so much drug abuse by her mother and her mother's so called "friends", that the idea held no allure for her. Briar sat up in bed, slowly pulling her knees up under her chin, and encircling them with both arms. She jerked her head sideways; refusing the joint in Brandon's outstretched hand. This obviously offended him, as he snapped, "You're a stuck up little trailer tramp." He reached into a paper bag on the floor between his feet, and pulled out a bottle of liquor, raising it to his lips. Taking a swig, he slurred, "I'm your fucking step-brother, and I'm just trying to be friendly, but you're being a little bitch! Here, take a drink, bitch." He shoved the neck of the bottle in her mouth, tipping it up at the same time. Briar spat it out while pushing the bottle away—spilling half of it down her front, and all over her pink eyelet bedspread. This further incensed Brandon, who was already stoned or drunk or both. He suddenly backhanded Briar so hard that she screamed before he could clap his hand over her mouth to silence her. Then, Brandon grabbed her left breast, squeezing it so hard that she began to cry as she tried to fight him off. He kept his hand on her mouth, and continued to squeeze her breast. Brandon's back was to the bedroom door, but over the top of his head, Briar saw the door open wide. The dim hall light revealed a small figure she recognized as Wesley, holding something long and shiny above his head. Wesley crossed the room in two strides, swinging the shiny object. Briar ducked as the object made direct contact with Brandon's face. The crushing blow knocked him backwards off the end of the bed. Briar jumped up and flipped on the overhead light. Brandon was struggling to his knees now, and bleeding profusely from his nose. Blood was gushing out onto her furry throw rug. Wesley stood over Brandon, holding Granddad's Masonic Ceremonial Sword. It always hung on the wall in her brothers' bedroom. Brandon grabbed at the sheathed sword to wrench it away, but ten year-old Wesley jerked upward, pulling the sword out of its sheath, then holding the sharp tip to Brandon's throat. In a low growl, Briar heard Wesley say, "Don't even think about it, fucker." Briar hadn't heard Wesley cuss before, and she had never seen him be so aggressive. Brandon rolled to the right, jumped up, and ran for the stairs. Wesley, sword in hand, followed in hot pursuit. Once Brandon reached the den and locked himself in, Wesley came back upstairs to Briar's room, where he slept alongside her for the rest of the night…never loosening his grip on the hilt of the sword.

Early the next morning, everyone was sitting at the breakfast table…everyone except for Brandon. Sarah banged on the locked den door, shouting for Brandon to come eat something. The den was directly adjacent to the kitchen, so when the door slowly opened—there stood Brandon, sporting two black eyes. Dried blood covered his swollen face, and was splattered down the front of his shirt. He clearly had a badly broken nose, as it was lying on one side of his face. Briar and Wesley exchanged startled glances, as Sarah screamed, and Mike quickly jumped up from the table. The kids sat there in silence, while Brandon choked out some lame story about using the upstairs bathroom and tripping down the stairs in the middle of the night—face crashing into the banister.

From that day on…the bond between Briar and Wesley could not be broken. He was her "hero," of that she had always been certain. As for Brandon—he never came near either of them again.

Chapter 14

Porter was a mass of tubing, wires, and alarms. Feeding tubes were stuck in one arm, while a saline drip was in the other, with even more tubes snaking their way under the light blanket. The smell of medicines and sick people tickled Briar's nose, making it twitch.

She touched Wesley on the shoulder and whispered, "Angel, wake up…we have to talk."

Wesley's eyes popped open, startled.

"Huh! …Porter?"

"No, it's me. Let's step out into the hall."

Briar went straight for the coffee machine, feeding it a dollar. She pulled a face at the selection: soup, tea, coffee, Ovaltine.

"*Ovaltine!* That stuff kills lab rats, doesn't it?" she said.

"Huh," Wesley said, yawning and rubbing the tiredness from his eyes.

She led the way over to an area of small tables and sat with her back to the entrance.

"It's been a bad twenty-four hours, little cousin of mine…and it's about to get a lot worse."

"What happened to your eyes, Briar? My God, who did that to you?" Wesley said, reaching out his hand.

"Don't touch; they're hurting like hell at the moment. Even so, the pain isn't nearly as bad as the pain I intend to inflict on the bastard that did it…once I finally get my hands on him."

"I don't need a psychic to tell me that the person who did this to you is the same psycho that tried to kill Porter. It's true, isn't it, Bri?"

"Yes, I think it's the same person. You won't believe what all has happened since I left you here last night…"

After twenty minutes of sharing all the details of the previous night, the funeral, and her encounter today with Kimo Kanoa—Briar sat back and tossed down the dregs of her watery coffee.

"So, my precious cousin, now you can see why I'm so stressed out and ready to run for cover. The guy that killed Craig has to be the same glitter-eyed *moke* that beat me up and did those horrible things to Porter. I know it. The first thing we need to do is find a safe place for us, somewhere that we can't be found, but still close enough that we can track this fucker down."

"We have a problem, Briar. Porter can't be moved for at least another twenty-four hours. The doctor was in an hour ago to say that the mega doses of Zyvox are taking care of the infection, but it could come back if we aren't careful."

"I don't think you understand; we need to get him and us out of here. The killer is coming as sure as sundown," Briar said, digging her nails into Wesley's hand.

"Jeremy…Jeremy Tuttle, that's his name," Wesley said, as he hugged himself and rocked back and forth. “Porter was having nightmares and calling out for Jeremy to stop…that it hurt…that he was killing him.” Wesley wiped at his eyes and continued to rock. “A few hours ago, he regained consciousness. I asked him who Jeremy was, and if it was Jeremy that had hurt him. He said yes, it was him…”

“He hurt me so bad, Wesley. He wouldn’t stop. I pleaded with him, but he just continued. I thought I’d be ripped apart. I’m so afraid; what if he finds me...?”

“He won’t find you, Porter, I’ll make sure. Tell me who he is, and where I can find him.”

“Jeremy Tuttle...”

“And then he passed out.” Wesley knuckled his eyes. “I have the bastard’s name; I’ll find him.”

“No, you are not going to find him. We are getting Porter out of here to somewhere safe. Once we’re safe, then I’ll take it from there.”

“Try to stop me, Briar. I’ll kill the fucker—I swear it!”

“Didn’t you hear anything I said a moment ago? This whole situation is like a Winnie the Pooh wasp nest about to explode. If this Tuttle is the killer (and I’m sure he is), he’s about to short-circuit and go on a killing spree. Porter has to be high on his list; he’s the only one that can recognize him.” She crumpled her paper cup, tossed it at a trash bin, and missed.

“But that’s not all…who’s paying Tuttle, who’s calling the shots, and why? This is going to get real ugly for a lot of people here on the Island. I’m talking old family people, if my hunch is right,” Briar said, biting her lower lip—something she always did when she was deep in thought. “It has to be Kalani Stanton or Jimmy Hinoko, two of the wealthiest families in Hawaii. The last thing you want to do is piss off a Hawaiian…or a Japanese. The question is, though, who would stand to gain the most from Craig’s death?”

Wesley sat slumped over, his chin on his chest, exhausted.

"I know a place we can go where we'll be safe; no one could ever find us," he whispered.

"Where's that, Wesley? Tell me quickly…the clock is ticking."

Chapter 15

Pearl City is a working class sprawl of middle-income homes built in the fifties and sixties that are rapidly being torn down and replaced with homes that are more modern. The newer dwellings are fetching much higher prices from more affluent buyers escaping from Honolulu's traffic and twenty-four hour a day tourist glut. Pearl City is a good place to live if you want to keep a low profile and go about your business without nosy neighbors or over-aggressive cops. It was the perfect place for Jeremy Tuttle to not be seen.

His reflection in the floor-to-ceiling mirrors that covered the gym's three main walls stared back at him. Tuttle was an ugly man; he knew it, and had always used it to his advantage. He especially enjoyed how it terrified his victims when they realized what was happening to them. His wide forehead sloped into bushy brows sitting on a tight pair of close-set eyes. The zigzag of the broken nose bone was his most prominent feature that he grooved on when people stared at. His tiny mouth was an afterthought, no more than a slash of red above a weak chin that disappeared into his muscled neck.

He liked looking at his body as he worked the weights. He was a mass of muscle with an intricately inked tattoo that covered his upper body and back. It had taken years for the tattoo to be finished; even now, the mouth of the creature lacked detail. One or two more visits under the needle and it would be finished, and he would be free; there would be nothing to hold him back.

Tuttle smiled at his reflection as he turned to admire his body. The tattooed creature's tail and body ran from the split in his butt cheeks up and over his shoulder and down his chest and abdomen, disappearing into his trunks. He nodded knowingly to himself; he and his victims were the only ones that knew where the tip of the tail emerged and where the lizard's tongue would end when finished. His choice of a lizard tattoo was a stroke of genius, especially the gecko. Geckos were camouflaged with bright colors that they could change at will, they were stealthy often waiting patiently for hours to strike their prey, and they were prolific little fuckers, multiplying every few weeks.

Others at the gym went out of their way to not get close to him; no one dared to ask the meaning of the tattoo. If they did ask, he ignored them. It was none of their frigging business; they wouldn't understand anyway. He didn't understand most of the time either anymore. His mind shifted at times from being Jeremy Tuttle, a retired fleet sailor, and then other times he was his mother, Dee. The separation of the two in his mind was becoming blurry, and he welcomed it. He thought of it as the day merging with the night, brightness to darkness, where he is permitted to do the thing that he loved to do most in the world, torture and kill. He wasn't sure why he enjoyed killing; he knew that it was wrong and there had to be some psycho-babble meaning to it, but he wasn't going to waste his time worrying about the *why* of it, he just wanted the *do* of it. The more his victims cried and begged, the more he hurt them; he loved it. The erotic euphoria it brought him was unimaginable, the orgasmic release staggering. However—down deep inside, where no one is permitted to see, was an even darker motivation. His sniveling old man. He was a coward…a weak caricature of a man…a spineless nothing for allowing a woman to destroy him. Jeremy was glad the old man killed himself in a fit of terror. Then there was Dee. Just the thought of Dee made his blood run hot. He hated the fucking bitch with all of his being for the way she had treated his father. She drove him to suicide; he died a pathetic and emasculated man. Father was never a strong man; in fact, he was almost fragile, which made it easier for Dee to physically abuse him. Many times while growing up, Jeremy witnessed his mother beat his father mercilessly with a belt or fists, knocking him to the floor, then kicking him unconscious. He killed Dee when he was eighteen. He beat her to death with a broomstick, then jammed it up her ass as far as it would go. Satisfied with his work, he went upstairs, masturbated, and slept the best he had in years. The next day, with his mother's body still on the kitchen floor, he went to the military recruiting offices in downtown Houston, joined the Navy, and never returned.

The tattoo was a present to himself after an extremely satisfying kill he had made while on liberty in Yokosuka, Japan. He was only a seaman first then, but powerfully built…strong enough to kill one of his shipmates with a single chop of his hand. By that point, the fun had been over anyway. The little shit was already cut and beaten so badly that it just took a whack of his hand to send him to La-La Land forever.

He rotated his head on its axis, stretching his neck muscles as he rolled his shoulders and arms in a rowing motion. The synchronized movement gave the illusion that the gecko's legs were moving in tandem, talons of dripping blood appeared to dig deeper, and the visible portion of the head seemed to move back and forth. Tuttle smiled at the quiet that fell over the gym.

The dinging of his cell phone interrupted his pleasure. Only two people had this number: Porter and his current benefactor, Mayor Bobby Hilo. He didn't want to talk to either at the moment; he was still deciding what to do about Porter and that bitch in the apartment last night.

"Yes," he said.

"Mr. Smith, is that you?" Mayor Bobby Hilo asked guardedly. He only knew Tuttle by the name Mr. Smith. He knew it was not the man's real name, but that was okay with him. The less he knew about this hired gun the better, *"Deniability, right, Bobby?"*

"Yes. Why are you calling? I told you to never call this number unless it was an emergency."

"Well, it is an emergency of sorts, Mr. Smith. We need to meet…tonight. I have a special problem that needs to be taken care of," he said nervously.

Mayor Hilo despised what he had become. He wondered how things had gotten to this point. He was disgusted with himself. Why did he ever listen to his fat pig of a wife and her constant nagging about how Craig Stanton had made millions as the senator from Hawaii? She shoved Stanton's name in his face every fucking day until he finally relented and agreed to run against Stanton in the upcoming election. He knew that he wasn't qualified and he didn't even want the position, but just to shut the bitch up, he agreed. Knowing that he was not popular as Mayor of Honolulu, he knew he would never win by running against the well-liked and charismatic Stanton. To win, he would have to get him out of the way, permanently. He visited his cousin, Kenny Kanoki, and asked him to find someone he could use to rough up a union boss who was giving him trouble. A few days later, Mr. Smith called him at his home, the job was explained, a fee settled on, and soon after…the job was complete.

Now that things were closing in on him, he needed to start erasing his tracks before it was too late and he was found out. His wife knew without him saying that he was connected somehow with Craig Stanton's murder. Just the knowing look on her face told him that he was owned. He would never be safe as long as she was around. Bobby wanted Mr. Smith to make his wife disappear…permanently.

"No. I told you in the beginning that we would never meet face-to-face. I know who you are and what you look like; that's all I need to know. You don't need to know anything about me," Tuttle said.

"This can't be discussed over the phone; we have to meet. I'll pay you double, but it has to be now, tonight."

Tuttle smiled; he was getting paid by this fucking idiot for something he would gladly do for free. It was also time to start closing a few doors.

"Meet me at Fort DeRussy Park on Waikiki at eleven. I'll be waiting at the flagpole. Be there with the money and come alone," Tuttle said and punched the End Call icon with a smile.

Tuttle squeezed his legs tight against the motorcycle's fuel tank and engine, enjoying the erection the powerful motor's vibration gave him. The cycle belonged to one of his kills from a few months earlier, some Dixie-cup deck ape stationed at Pearl. The little shit didn't even put up a fight. *"Hey, to the victor go the spoils, ain't that right? Fucking-A, they do."*

He dropped off H-1 at Ala Moana and took back streets to DeRussy, the Army's recreation park for service members on liberty or leave from Pacific-rim duty stations. This time of night, the park was quiet with most of the light coming from the brilliant moon above. He parked the big cycle next to a handicapped spot and walked slowly down the path leading to the beach. He sensed others around him, but wasn't concerned; the park at night was often used by couples for making out. He had used the park as a rendezvous point also in the past, for quick liaisons. That was back when his gratification needs were simpler; now he needed space to work in. He chuckled at referring to what he loved as *work. "A man should love what he does, ha, ha."*

Tuttle circled the meeting spot several times, watching for a trap. The fat-fuck mayor was sitting on a bench directly under a lamppost, fidgeting and wiping his brow with a lank hanky.

"Mayor," he called out. "Over here, hands where I can see them."

Mayor Hilo jumped at the voice coming from a cluster of Hibiscus bushes. "Is that you, Mr. Smith?"

"Shut up, ya fat fuck. No names, now get over here or I'm gone."

Tuttle grabbed the mayor and began to search him for a weapon or wire. He didn't trust the little prick, and wasn't going to get tripped up this close to his coming-out day.

"Hey, what are these?" he grinned and squeezed the mayor's balls hard.

"Oow! That hurts, let go," Hilo whined in pain.

Tuttle laughed as he pulled a thick envelope from the mayor's waistband. He thumbed through the stack of bills, licking his lips and feeling a tingle low in his pelvis.

"Whoa! Who you want me to kill, Bobby? Is Obama coming for an early vacation?" he laughed. He loved Obama, but for this kind of bread, he wouldn't give it a second thought.

"No, no, worse. I want you to…to…do my wife, you know, do her," he mumbled.

Tuttle was caught off-guard. "You want me to screw your wife?"

"Don't be obtuse, Mr. Smith. You know very well what I mean." Even though Hilo hated his wife, just the thought of this psycho mating with her was repulsive. My God, there are limitations, aren't there?

Tuttle was quick to grasp the good fortune that had just fallen in his lap. He needed money and mobility if he and Dee were to do their thing, and this fuck just handed him a golden egg.

"Your Honor, the good news is that I accept the job, the bad news is that it's going to cost a hundred grand."

"*What!* A hundred grand? Are you crazy? …Uh, sorry. You can't be serious. A hundred thousand dollars for a wife?"

"Keep yapping and it goes to one-fifty."

"But…but, I don't have that kind of money," he stammered.

"Find it, or I'll start squealing like a newborn shoat."

"You bastard. You don't have anything on me. If you go to the cops, you'll trip yourself up. You are crazy, Smith..."

Tuttle grabbed a handful of hair and pulled the rotund man in close. Hilo lost his balance, but remained upright in pain.

"Let go, let go, don't hurt me," he screamed.

Tuttle opened his mouth wide and chomped down on Hilo's shoulder muscle. He bit into the flesh, jerking his head sharply back and forth, then just as quickly, he released his hold.

"You little shit, you'll do as I say. Bring me one hundred thousand by this time tomorrow night, or I'll shove that fat body of yours into a wood chipper and let it grind you up into little pieces."

Hilo fell to his knees as Tuttle released him. Blood darkened the front of his colorful shirt as he held his hand to the wound.

“I don’t have that kind of money lying around. I need at least a few days to sell some stock…”

“Eleven tomorrow night, or you die, fat man,” Tuttle snarled. “Don’t even think of setting a trap for me; just remember, if I go down, you go down.”

Tuttle cocked his head, listening. The park had fallen silent. The only sound was a gecko chirping; he smiled and faded into the shadows.

The cycle started up effortlessly as he straddled the tank and squeezed. “Oh, yeah, giddy-up cowboy,” he said. “Now, let’s go find out what that bitch was doing in Porter’s apartment last night.”

Chapter 16

The elevator whispered quietly as it sped up to the fifteenth floor. Briar was tired, hungry, and needed a shower. She needed all three, but sleep was winning out over the other two. She flipped on the master lights as she closed the door behind her. The apartment smelled of pine cleanser and blood, a smell she had first experienced on a field trip with the Agency to the National Body Farm in Tennessee. She still gagged at the staggering number of bodies placed around the farm in different poses, and left to decompose.

The agent-trainees were taught how to recognize mitigating factors from the different stages of decomposition: how long the corpse had been there, the different bugs that feast on the decaying flesh at different phases over time, color variations, types of wounds and injuries that may have contributed to the death. Since most of the cadavers were unclaimed homeless or wards of the state, the wounds and injuries were made at the farm when a shipment of the dead arrived from around the country. She watched as a smirking deputy fired a double load of buckshot into an emaciated wino's corpse, and then threw up when the chest disintegrated. She knew the smell well.

She stopped by the fridge for a quick look, and just as quickly closed it as a whiff of something spoiled hit her. Breathing through her mouth, she made it into Auntie Cyd's master bedroom and collapsed on the down comforter. In seconds, she was in a deep troubled sleep.

Multicolored streamers waved and beckoned as the wind filled the room with music. U2 was singing a song from her childhood, something about not finding what I'm looking for. She tried to remember the name, but couldn't. The wind howled, suddenly changing the room into a cyclone of faces from her past; her biological mother Donna flashed by, laughing, as she bared her sharpened teeth. Wesley was crouched in a corner screaming fearfully for her to run, to get out, but she didn't understand.

"Wake up, pretty girl; wake up, we need to talk."

Briar's eyes flew open and she started to scream, but a calloused hand clamped across her mouth.

"Careful, my pretty, or Uncle Jeremy will snap your scrawny neck," Tuttle said, leaning close into Briar's face.

Briar fought and bucked, trying to get the weight off of her chest. Her terrified mind was screaming.

"Tuttle…Tuttle…Tuttle…Have to get away…Have to get away."

Tuttle's breath made her gag; his animal guttural moaning was petrifying. As she continued to buck, her right hand found his crotch, and she squeezed. Tuttle screamed in agony as she milked her hand, squeezing with all her strength with each new grasp.

Tuttle rolled off of her, holding his crotch.

“You fucking bitch; I swear, you’re dead meat.”

Briar flipped off the bed and crab crawled across the room. At the door, she scrambled to her feet and ran into the kitchen. She couldn’t remember where she had left her purse. She needed the gun inside. She grabbed a carving knife out of the block holder and ran back into the bedroom, determined to kill Tuttle. She hated this animal with all of her being. She would kill him for what he did to Craig and Porter, and to her last night. He was waiting for her. As she ran into the room, he side-kicked her in the leg, knocking her down. He was on her in a flash, pinning her to the floor.

“Talk to me, bitch. Where’s the old fag?” he demanded through gritted teeth.

Briar's leg was throbbing. Through the pain, she puckered a ball of saliva and spit in Tuttle's face. “Go to hell, Tuttle,” she hissed.

“Ah-ha, she knows my name,” he said. “Tsk tsk, little lady, there's no getting out of here alive now. You know my name. Did the old fag tell you what he called me? Did he?”

Tuttle was lying on top of Briar, holding her arms out, spread-eagle, face-to-face. She tried to move, but he had her pinned.

“He called me his big papaya, ha, ha. You want to know why?”

“Screw you, Tuttle. I’ll kill you if I get up…so you better kill it now…if you’re *man* enough. But you’re scared of women, aren’t you? Have mommy issues, do we? Did she dress you up like a girl, Jeremy?” she taunted, trying to make him lose his temper and give her an opening.

It worked. Tuttle head-butted Briar on the forehead. She lost consciousness. After a few moments, she came to, gasping; she couldn't breathe. Tuttle had a strong grip on her throat; he was choking her, trying to collapse her esophagus, and his fingers were digging into the back of her neck, pushing on the vertebrae. Her vision was beginning to dim, the air in her lungs was gone…he was killing her.

Her mind flashed back to a fight she had with a crack-crazed bitch in the Bronx, who she was trying to serve divorce papers on. The woman was stop-sign thin, with a huge head of wiry yellow hair, and a mouth full of rotten teeth from the acid in the crack. When Briar, standing on the stoop six steps up from street level, revealed the purpose of the visit—the woman went ballistic. Without warning, she hit Briar with a bony fist, knocking her backwards off the stoop. Briar's fall resembled a slalom ride down the steps. Pain shot up her back as it made contact with each step. The woman dove from the top of the stoop, through the air, landing squarely on top of Briar…and proceeded to strangle her. The woman's face was inches away from hers, the fetid breath from the rotted teeth gagged Briar as she struggled to free herself. An image of Hazel the Witch flashed across her mind, harkening back to the orphanage and the old cook Hazel, who all the kids were terrified of. Darkness was rimming her eyesight when she remembered two boys fighting over her…

Remembering gave her a sudden burst of strength, as she jabbed two fingers deep into Tuttle's right eye. He screamed, let go of her throat, and fell away holding his eye socket. Briar rolled away, scooped up the carving knife, and drove it into Tuttle's back. He groaned and fell forward with one hand on his bloody eye socket, and the other reaching for the knife handle over his shoulder.

Briar backed away, turned around, and ran—snatching up her purse from the coffee table as she passed…then out the front door to the elevator lobby. Her fingers were shaking as she stabbed at the down button. A hundred years went by before the elevator doors slid open. Briar wanted to throw up from fear. She wiped bloody snot from her nose as she searched her bag for Wesley's gun that she'd taken from his room a lifetime ago. The doors were sliding closed when her hand gripped the pistol butt, and she pointed out into the landing lobby. The ride down was interminable. She tried to calm her shaking hands, her breathing was ragged, and she was light headed from the chokehold, but at least she was alive.

Chapter 17

Briar ran down the middle of the street in her bare feet, dodging water puddles, glass, and stones. Every few steps, she would look over her shoulder to see if Tuttle was behind, chasing her. A car sped by, the driver leaned on his horn and shouted as he flashed his lights, "*Ya crazy bitch, get out of the street.*"

"*Fuck you!*" Briar shouted back and raised the pistol in her hand. "What are you doing, Briar? Put that away before you shoot someone," she said to herself.

She had to get control of herself and get some place safe in case Tuttle did come after her. There was an all-night noodle shop two blocks over, and she ran for it, gripping the pistol tightly.

Ichi Bon Soba was packed with Japanese newlyweds, all enjoying bowls of noodles and talking loudly. Briar pulled the door open, turned to watch for Tuttle, and backed into the shop. The place fell silent immediately at the sight of the redheaded *gaijin* with blood all over her front.

"*What?*" Briar shouted at the blank faces.

She caught a glimpse of herself in the mirror behind the counter and understood their reaction to her appearance.

"Sorry," she said apologetically, and hurried to the ladies room. She closed the stall door, slid the lock in place, and sat. Her mind was numb.

"This is no way to enjoy Hawaii," she mumbled.

Someone in the next stall coughed politely and then was quiet.

Briar's thoughts were beginning to spin down from terror mode to just-scared mode when she pulled Detective Kimo Kanoa's business card from the side pocket of her purse. She punched his number into her phone and waited.

"Bettah be good, *brah*," Kimo answered wearily.

"Sergeant Kanoa, this is Briar Malone; I need help. The killer is Jeremy Tuttle. He's in my apartment right now. He just tried to murder me…"

"Whoa, *sistah*, slow it down, you're not making sense. Who's trying to kill you? Where are you?"

"I'm sitting in the *binjo* at Ichi Bon Soba, hiding from Jeremy Tuttle. Tuttle is the 'killer', Kimo. He beat me up last night, and nearly killed me again tonight, but I stabbed him. I know I didn't kill him; he's still alive and in my apartment. I'm scared, Kimo."

"Okay, give me twenty minutes; stay at the noodle shop. I'll hook a ride with a patrol car. Give me your address again and I'll have a couple of cops sit on the place until we get there."

"Bring a fucking bazooka; he's huge."

A few minutes later, Briar was washing her face, trying to get the blood off, when the door opened and a small woman entered.

“You leave. Customers upset, they complain about you; they say you dangerous American. No want trouble, they say, ‘Hands up, no shoot,’ like on television in U.S.A.”

“What the…oh jeeze louise!” Briar said, as it dawned on her, the woman was making reference to *Ferguson, MO, and Michael Brown.*

“Customers. They say they come Hawaii for Paradise, not want be killed by pa hula wahini.”

“*I am not a crazy white woman! Well, I’m white, and I am a little crazy at the moment, but have some compassion please – I’m obviously in distress here*,” Briar said, and spit blood into the sink.

“You go, or I call police.”

Briar cupped her hand with water and swished it around in her mouth. The old woman motioned for someone to come to her.

A teenage boy dressed in cook’s whites stuck his head in, and said, “My mom says you have to leave or she's calling the cops." He tried to sound tough, but failed. "Let's move it, lady." He grabbed Briar's arm and yanked.

Briar lost it. She was tired of people hitting and shoving her around; she'd had enough *macho bullshit* for one night.

With a surge of adrenaline, Briar whipped the kid around, twisting his arm up behind his back and pinning him against the grimy bathroom door. "Look, you little punk, I've had enough shit for one day. Thanks for your hospitality, but I believe I'll wait for my ride outside."

Briar released her grip on his arm, and shoved the kid toward his squealing mother, both of whom *beat feet* back to the kitchen. Briar moved slowly toward the front door, making deliberate eye-contact with as many of the Japanese patrons as she could. She backed out of the shop, then turned and crossed the street to wait for Kimo.

Briar was sitting on the curb in a grand funk. She had never felt so low; her head pounded to the beat of her heart, her eyes were swollen and black, her nose was clogged with blood, and her jaw throbbed. Aunt Cyd's dress was ruined: bloodstained, and torn. She didn't have any idea where the hat was; the last she remembered wearing it was at Craig's funeral. My God, was that just a few hours ago? The penthouse was a disaster area. The Keane painting was possibly a total loss. There might be a man lying in a pool of blood (dead, she hoped) in Auntie's bedroom. How was she going to explain all of this? Briar shuddered at the thought of Arturo and his new bride-to-be arriving in Honolulu in less than fifteen hours. She had to call her Aunt and tell her the truth about what was happening. Meanwhile, she feared what Tuttle would do to her the next time they met.

Mano pulled the plain-wrap cop car to the curb, shining the bright headlights on Briar.

“Cut the lights, damn it,” Briar yelled, as she shielded the glare with her forearm. “Knock it off.”

As he jumped out of the car to assist her, Kimo asked “Miss Malone, how badly are you hurt?” He was shocked at her beaten face. “Shoots Mano, let’s get her to Queen’s E.R. fast.” He almost didn’t recognize Briar in her disheveled condition, and without the big sunglasses and hat that she’d worn earlier at the funeral, but he did recognize the dress and the red hair.

“Forget the E.R.; we need to catch Tuttle before he gets away.” Briar protested.

Briar allowed Kimo to help her up from the curb; her aching muscles screamed at the effort. *She was suddenly so tired and wanted to close her eyes for a few minutes…then she would be all right. She felt safer now that Kimo was there…he would watch over her…Tuttle couldn’t get to her…not with Kimo and Mano…we are all safe now…*Briar blacked out.

Her eyes popped open and she sat up, startled, swiveling her head around, and trying to get a fix on where she was. The last she remembered, she was sitting on the curb waiting for Kimo to show. She was in a hospital, the bedside tray and the I.V. drip were a giveaway, and the awful smell of sickness gagged her. She threw the sheet back and threw her legs off the side of the bed—immediately collapsing backwards in a vertigo spin. She gripped the mattress tightly, holding on until the dizziness stopped.

"Nurse! I need help here," she called out.

A giant of a man in a Police uniform hustled in, hand on his holster.

"What is it, Miss Malone?" he said, looking around the room for intruders.

"Let me guess, Kimo found Tuttle's body in my apartment and booked me on a murder charge."

"No, Ma'am. I don't know anything about a Tuttle, but I can tell you for sure that you are not booked on anything. Detective Kanoa told me to stand outside your room until he returns," he said, checking his watch.

"So, I'm free to go."

"Uh, I don't know. I was told to not let anyone in, except the doctor and the nurses, but he didn't say anything about you leaving."

"Call a nurse for me, please," Briar said, as she pressed the call button. "I need to get this I.V. out and get my own clothes on. I'm getting out of here."

"I'm sorry, Miss Malone," a nurse said as she entered the room. "Doctors orders are bed rest for twenty-four hours." She pushed Briar back down and pulled the sheets up to her neck.

"Wrong. I'm out of here—please, just get this needle out of my arm," Briar said, turning her head away in anticipation of pain.

"No, Ma'am, you're not going anywhere; now *you* lie back down and just relax. You're exhausted and need rest," the nurse said, as she injected something into the drip line, which Briar assumed was a sedative.

"The last thing I have time for right now is bed rest; now move out of my way," Briar said, as she tore the tape off her forearm and pulled the needle out of the bruised vein. "Ouch—dammit."

The nurse stood back, turned, and rushed out the door toward the nurse's station. "We have a Code Yellow in 104," she called out.

The police officer was at a loss, "Whe…where you going?"

"Do you have a car outside?"

"Yes, Ma'am," he stuttered.

"Pull it around and wait for me; I'll be right out."

"But…"

"Kanoa told you to protect me, didn't he?"

"Yes, Ma'am."

"Well, I need protecting! Now, pull that freaking car around."

Briar locked the bathroom door and stripped off the hospital gown. She held up Aunt Cyd's ruined dress, sighed, and tossed it across the room into the trash can. She rummaged through the small closet and found a pair of pajama bottoms and pulled them on. She slipped her feet into a pair of paper slippers. The *coup de gras* was the hospital gown, which she turned around backwards, crossing the tails at the waist, and tying them tightly behind her back.

A young doctor followed her out the door, insisting that she remain under his care. A nurse, close behind, waved a clipboard demanding that she sign a waiver.

Briar ignored them both and jumped into the waiting patrol car.

"What's your name, big guy?" Briar asked the cop.

"Eddie Aikau," he answered.

"Okay, Eddie Aikau, call me Briar. Stop at the first convenience store you see; I need to eat something before I pass out."

"Should I call Detective Kanoa, Miss Briar? I think this is beyond my orders from him."

"No, please don't bother Detective Kanoa; this is not a life threatening situation—I just need a ride to my destination." Briar tried to sound casual.

Eddie pulled into an ABC store, cutting the engine.

Briar already had one leg out of the car before it came to a stop, saying, "I'm getting some energy bars and a coffee, what do you want?"

"That works for me too," Eddie said.

Eddie knew he should give Kimo a "heads up" to let him know what was going on, but thought better of it. He had been in on the quick briefing Kimo gave the lieutenant over the phone, when he and Mano brought Briar into the E.R. Besides being Kimo's cousin, Eddie had idolized

Kimo since he was a kid. He always wanted to be a cop like his *cuz*, and after his discharge from the Marines, the department snapped him up. That was eleven years ago, and Eddie was still a basic patrol officer—catching all the shit jobs that they could throw at him. Now was his chance to prove he was capable of more than working foot patrol at Ala Moana Mall. Briar Malone was a person of interest in the Senator Craig Stanton murder. He was going to stick with her and bust her if she slipped up. A plan formulated in his mind quickly shifted to a daydream in which he would ask innocent, but probing questions that could trip her up. If it worked…Aloha Ala Moana.

Briar handed Eddie two coffees and a bag of bars through the car window, as she said, "Wait here."

Briar went behind the store, quickly switching into a cotton T-shirt, and tossing the hospital gown into a dumpster. The first shirt she grabbed off the rack featured a silkscreened marijuana plant, with Pakalolo imprinted above it, and Kona Gold beneath. What the heck…when in Rome. Neither a toker nor a smoker, Briar appreciated the irony, as she slid back into the car—grabbing her coffee and ripping open an energy bar.

"Jump back on H-1, Eddie."

"Where we going, Miss Briar?"

"Hale´iwa, and step on it."

"The North Shore? We goin' surfing, lady? Who's over there dat you know anyway?"

"Just my Precious Angel. Now punch it, Eddie."

Chapter 18

Slivers of sunlight were shooting over the western horizon as Eddie rolled up into the sparse front yard on Papua Street in Hale'iwa. The wood-frame house was identical to fifty others just like it, once he got off H-1.

"You sure this is it?" he said.

"It's the only one with a Harley in the yard; this has to be it."

Just to be sure, Briar hit Wesley's cell number. They sat in silence, waiting for him to pick up. The heat tic from the car's engine was the only nearby sound in the predawn light; a rooster crowed far off in the hills overlooking the town. The roar of the ocean was such a constant that it wasn't even noticed.

"Are you here?" Wesley said sleepily.

"I'm not sure. Come out on the front porch and I'll tell you if I'm here or not," Briar said.

Wesley appeared on the covered porch, stretching and yawning. He saw the car, and called out, “Hey, I knew you wouldn’t get lost. I never give bad directions. Come on in; we have the place to ourselves for the moment, but leave the *fuzz* in the car.”

“I’m going in with you, Briar. I don’t know this guy; he might try something. I’m still responsible for you.”

“This is the end of the line for you and me, Eddie. It’s been fun; now get on back to Honolulu before you get into big trouble.”

“Sorry, Briar, no can do—I’m sticking with you. Otherwise, Kimo will have my dick on a stick, pardon the expression.”

“Suit yourself, but you’ll have to stay out in the car while I talk privately with my *cuz*,” Briar said. As she opened the car door, she turned back, handing Eddie a twenty. “I’m still hungry—would you be a *mensch*, and go back down to the highway to the Jack in the Box we passed, and pick us up a few breakfast meals?"

"That sounds good to me. That energy bar, she not go far."

"Take your time, Eddie."

Wesley met Briar at the door with coffee in one hand and a hot towel in the other.

"Sit over here and let me look at that face. If you keep getting that gorgeous *punam* of yours bashed in, you're going to have a tough time finding someone who'll want you," he joked.

"Where is Porter?" she asked, pulling out a chair from the small kitchen table.

The house was small, but neat and clean in a male sort of way. It belonged to Wesley's friend, Sharkey Dolin, a *haole* from Houston going way back. Sharkey moved to Oahu with a friend several years ago. When they weren't working odd jobs, they surfed. Wesley drove around the island every few months to watch different world-class surfers compete in International Open events. Sharkey usually placed top ten of the competitions he participated in. Wesley was a pretty good surfer himself, but not world-class by any stretch of the imagination.

“Sharkey is babysitting Porter at the hospital. Porter’s fever hit the roof around two this morning and we rushed him over to General on this side of the Island. When I got your call shortly after that, I hurried back here to meet you.”

“Is he going to be all right?”

“The truth?” Wesley said. “How can someone be so badly damaged internally and live? I can’t let myself dwell on it too much, but if he dies, I won’t rest until Tuttle is dead. I’ll do it with my own hands, even if it means prison, Briar. I will somehow get my revenge on that twisted mo’fo.”

“Wesley, I don’t know how we’ve managed to get ourselves in the middle of this mess, but we are up to our necks. We don’t need to go down any further. I would love to beat the man to death with a stick myself, for all the pain and suffering he's caused, but realistically…we just need to get him behind bars before he hurts someone else."

"I know where he lives, Bri."

"What? How do you know that?" she said, pushing the towel away from her face.

"Porter told me. Sharkey, Jones, and I were going to pay him a visit once it was safe to leave Porter alone. Now that he's tucked away in the hospital, and safe with Sharkey—I say we do a slow drive-by and see if we can flush him out."

Briar liked the idea. The idea she liked even better was to somehow get Tuttle to confess who hired him to kill Craig. She didn't have any idea how the two of them could subdue Tuttle, unless they caught him off-guard. She knew that the really smart thing to do would be to tell Detective Kanoa where they could find Tuttle and let the police "sweat it out of him" who he'd been hired by. But then, how could she be confident that

Tuttle would talk? No…she needed to see this one through herself. After all, it was her name and reputation on the line. If she planned on staying in the security field, she couldn't have any suspicion of criminality or wrongdoing on her record. The state licensing was very strict on granting Private Investigator permits, especially if there was even a hint of impropriety. Just trying to explain her early FBI years would be hard enough; she didn't need a Person of Interest rap to further complicate those future employment prospects.

"I need a quick shower and a clean pair of pants…then we'll roll on Tuttle."

"Most of Shark's clothing would be too big for you, but Jones might have something that will fit," Wesley said, smiling at the potential for retribution over what he'd selected for Bri to wear.

"What are you grinning about, Wesley Barrett? I know that smart-ass smirk means trouble."

"Don't worry, honey; you'll see."

When Briar got out of the shower and toweled off, she felt better than she had in—days? This was only her third day on the Island, but it seemed more like months. She focused on what needed to be done once they cornered Tuttle in his lair. They would verify that he was home, and then bring Kimo and his crew in to make the actual bust. She had gone through enough physical pain over the last few days to last her a lifetime. There was no way she was going to let Wesley get himself hurt either. Enough was enough…

The chime of her cell phone brought her back, "Good morning, Detective Kanoa," she said as she answered. "I was expecting your call hours ago; you must be on Island time."

"Knock off the funny stuff, Miss Malone. Where are you and where is my officer?"

"I'm in a much safer place than the E.R. at Queens, but I appreciate your effort," Briar said. "Officer Aikau is doing a great job protecting me, thank you very much. Did you know that he worships you…?"

"Cut out the chitchat and tell me where you are. Wherever it is, *YOU* are not safe. You shouldn't have left the hospital without notifying me. Tuttle's body wasn't in your apartment; he left behind a lot of blood but no 'body.' Chances are, he's looking for you to finish the job he started."

"I'm with a friend in Hale'iwa…," she started to say.

"Hale'iwa! Dammit, Briar—what are you doing over there? Did Eddie drive you? I'm going to have that *kanaka's 'okole…*"

"No, you're not, Kimo. I forced him to bring me here. I told him that if he called you, I would yell rape (or something). He is a sweetheart, Kimo; you really need to get him off mall security."

"Put him on the phone," Kimo said, perturbed.

“He’s not here at the moment; he ran an errand for me and should be back in a few minutes.”

“What kind of errand? He’s a uniformed officer for Christ’s sake; he’s not supposed to be running errands for civilians,” he fumed.

“We have to eat, Kimo. Eddie just ran down the street to get us some food. Don’t get your panties in a wad, okay?”

Briar smiled at the spluttering fit coming across the airwaves. She gave him a moment to get himself under control, and said,

“When he gets back, I’ll have him call you, but promise you won’t be hard on him, he’s your biggest fan.”

“You need to come back to Honolulu, Briar. I wasn’t kidding when I said you’re in danger. Tuttle trashed your penthouse on his way out, breaking lamps, chairs, coffee table, everything. The kitchen is a shambles, and the master bedroom…forget about it. I have it cordoned off as a crime scene, and I've got the lab boys taking prints and blood samples. I want to get a positive I.D., so there's no way he can get away."

"Kimo, I'm safe. I'm with my cousin Wesley and I trust him with my life. So, pull Eddie off...and give the kid a break."

"I can't force you to come back, Miss Malone. All I can legally do is to warn you. I'll say it again to make myself perfectly understood. We are dealing with a serial sexual predator that kills because he has to, not just because he wants to. Do you catch the difference between the two, Briar?"

"I know firsthand what you're talking about, Kimo. Believe me, I have no intention of being caught unawares again," she said sincerely. "I'll tell you what, I'll check in with you every few hours, just to let you know that I'm okay. If you don't hear from me after four or five hours, send Eddie to find me."

Briar hung up before Kimo could challenge her. She found clean clothes laid out for her on the bed and laughed. Wesley knew she liked leather, but what she slipped on were a pair of scuffed up leather biker pants, studs and all. She laughed again as she looked in the mirror hung from the closet door. Other than being a little baggy in the rear, they actually fit her pretty well. The black T-shirt with the skull and crossbones printed on the back fit tight across the chest in a sexy sort of way, but the sleeveless leather vest seemed a little over the top, even for Briar.

"Wesley, you brat. Check out the biker babe," she laughed, as she swished her way across the living room.

"Fabulous, dahling, simply fabulous," he said, punching the air. "I'm not sure how the flip-flops are going to go with the whole look, but those belong to his 8 year-old niece, and are the only footwear I could find that will fit your toy feet."

"*Slippahs*, how perfect! I'll be 'Briar the Banzai Beach Biker Bitch.' Wanted poster to read,

'Be on the lookout for a biker broad with neon red hair and lime green flip-flops.' Who wouldn't be intimidated by that alleged image?" Briar laughed.

"Cute, real cute, Briar. The first thing we need to do when we get back to civilization is to get you a new outfit. For now, that get-up is better that those pajama bottoms and that oversized Kona Gold T-shirt you arrived wearing. Just leave that stuff here for Sharkey."

After thirty minutes, Eddie hadn't returned. Briar's guess was that cousin Kimo got him on the horn and chewed a chunk out of his behind. Poor Eddie had probably seen the last of patrol duty; it was back to being *Paul Blart Mall Cop.*

"Guess I'll flip you to see who drives the bike and who rides bitch," Briar said, pointing to the shiny Harley out front.

"No way, Sharkey would kill me if we took *Shakira*. We'll make our way to Oz in the truck parked out back. Sharkey said I could use it as long as I put some gas in it."

Chapter 19

It was slow-going on the way back to Honolulu. Tourists in rental cars were especially dangerous as they weaved in and out around slower cars, or came to a complete stop for a selfie-moment with the ocean in the background. Bicyclists and backpackers all seemed to have a death wish. They waited until the last second before stepping off the pavement to safety, many shouting profanities and flipping the finger. Wesley had a demonic gleam in his eye, as he too would hold off till the last second and then blast the horn, scaring the hell out of unsuspecting targets.

"Wesley, you're going to kill one of those people. This is a pick-up truck, not your Vette," Briar said, as she white-knuckled the armrest. Crazy driving ran in the family, it seemed, but each one thought they were a better driver than the others.

“I’m just having a little fun, Bri. I’ve been through hell the last couple of days and need to blow off some of this rage.”

“Oh fuck,” Briar screamed. “I nearly forgot to tell you! Speaking of rage, Auntie Cyd arrives this afternoon. What in the hell are we going to tell her? This might be pushing her unconditional love to the point of ‘conditional’.”

Briar was sinking back into her funk. The leather pants made her itch, she’d left her sunglasses in the patrol car, her swollen eyes wouldn’t stop watering, and the waxy power bars she gobbled down earlier had given her indigestion.

“We’d better book a couple of rooms somewhere quick for her and Arturo. There is no way she’s getting across the crime scene tape at the penthouse. I don’t even want her to see it right now, if we can possibly avoid it.”

“Bri, just come clean with her and tell her everything that has happened. None of this is our fault—in fact we are all 'victims' of this maniac. Sorry I won't be around for the explosion."

"Uh-uh, no way, Wesley. You are the one who's going to have to tell her, not me. I just came back here to clear my name. The destruction to the apartment happened because Tuttle was trying to find Porter, and I got in the way, becoming *collateral damage*. This is on YOU buddy, for not vetting your boyfriends better. In fact, if I thought I could sue you for mental anguish, I would, cousin or not."

"There is no way I'm going to tell her on my own, Bri; you at least need to be there for moral support."

It occurred to Briar that telling Auntie might work in her favor. She hated to lie to Wesley, but these were desperate times. A plan formulated in her mind as they sped past Hanauma Bay toward Diamond Head.

By the time they passed Kahala, she was ready to spring her faux trap.

“Wesley, you know I love you more than anything in the world, don’t you?”

“Uh oh, I don’t like the tone of your voice. What are you up to Briar?”

“Nothing. I was just thinking that it really is my duty to tell Auntie Cyd about everything. Coming from me, she’ll take it a lot easier than if you told her.”

“I don’t like where this is going, Briar. I smell a red-headed rat,” Wes said suspiciously.

“Oh, come on, Angel, you know it would be easier on her if it came from me rather than you.”

“Okaaaay,” he stretched the word out doubtfully.

“Look, let’s make this simple. I’ll drop you off at the Royal Hawaiian and you can get a couple of rooms for Auntie and what’s-his-face, since they obviously can’t stay at the penthouse. I’ll run out to the airport to meet them and tell her the whole story.”

"I like it. I think that's an excellent plan, Bri. I'll also get you and me each a room, and we can all sit around tonight sipping adult beverages and singing *Kumbaya*. Truly brilliant plan my dear," he crowed, happy at getting off the hook.

"Swell, it's decided then. Now, let's swing by Nordstrom's at Ala Moana for something decent to wear," Briar said. "I'm sure I won't appear too suspicious, dressed and looking like this. What's the expression, rode hard and put away wet—well I'm all of that AND a bag of chips. Which reminds me—I'm still hungry! That little prick Eddie made off with my last twenty bucks."

As Wesley wandered around the men's department picking out a few things to hold him over until they could get back into the penthouse, Briar did some serious quick shopping of her own. In the dressing room, she changed into cargo shorts and a tank top, leaving the biker duds hanging there, for anyone that wanted them. She casually glanced at herself in the mirror as she mentally inventoried the purchases she'd just made to get her through a few days. Day and evening clothes, basic lingerie, and two pair of sandals—both of which she could *sprint* in, if necessary. A pair of Tom Ford sunglasses, a small bottle of Cocoa Noir perfume, and a jar of La Prairie Skin Caviar, for her traumatized face…list complete.

Back in the beat up truck, Wesley and Briar commented on each other's purchases. Both were slaves to fashion and loved to shop together. As children, Aunt Cyd took them with her on major shopping trips and taught them that quality always trumped trends. Just as class and style always won out over the mundane. *"Good taste can't be bought; you either have it or you don't,"* Cyd would admonish. She also taught them that money should never be an obstacle when dressing, *"If you want to look like a fishmonger's wife, buy from the chain stores. Otherwise, good fashion costs."*

"Now where to, *Cuz*?" Wesley asked.

"Drop me at the penthouse garage and I'll pick up my car. You go to the hotel and book us all in. Meanwhile, I'll head to the airport and wait for the lovers to land."

"You've made my day, Briar. Thank you for keeping me out of the direct line of fire. I know that Auntie would come around and eventually forgive me, but not before she chewed my ass up one side and down the other. I owe you one."

Wesley dropped Briar off on the corner and she made her way to the building's underground parking area undetected. She kept a sharp eye out for Tuttle, just in case he was lying in wait for her. That was silly, though, since he didn't know her car from a camel. She blamed her jitters on the shadowy light in the basement garage and the chill that always seemed to be present in these types of structures.

The Vette started up with a growl, and quickly settled down to a mellow rumble. The vibration through the seat always gave Briar the sensation that she had just strapped on four hundred horsepower of beast. A slight tap of the gas pedal and this baby would lunge. She giggled, thinking that driving a Corvette was probably the second best feeling in the world.

Chapter 20

She drove up the ramp onto H-1 and sped towards Pearl City. Her trick had been to get Wesley safely out of the danger zone as she did the snooping on Tuttle's creepy nest. Wesley was slow to anger and rarely revealed what he was really thinking to others. He always had a smile on his face, but inside he may be thinking how many pieces he was going to tear you into. Coming out of Nordstrom's she saw something in his demeanor that concerned her. Maybe it had been the sunlight or a reflection, but his eyes appeared to flash a brilliant green hue, and then it was gone. Briar knew her cousin like a book, but after that, she couldn't take the chance that she could control him if he got close to Tuttle. Keeping him tucked away at the Royal Hawaiian was a stroke of genius, while she poked around and reported anything interesting to Detective Kanoa. Once she did a quick reconnaissance, she would zip over to the airport and meet Auntie Cyd and Arturo.

Pearl City was just like any other small town where a bigger city had slopped over its boundaries, and you never really knew when you left one and entered the other. In the case of P.C., it was apparent within two blocks of entering that it was a working class town. This is where the people lived that kept the bigger city alive and breathing. The streets were not as well kept, nor the cars that puttered along those streets as new, or the people as happy and smiling as in the bigger city to the east. Briar thought the people looked depressed and tired, just getting by day-to-day with payday the only break in the tedium.

At times, she thought a simpler quiet life would suit her, maybe settle down, have a couple of kids, and then…and then what? That's as far as her thoughts of a simple life ever went. No, she needed more than a new car every few years, or Tuesday lunches with girlfriends. She needed…no, she actually *craved* excitement! Living on the edge, the rush of adrenaline. She called this her *Donna legacy*. The life and death urgency of being pursued by someone that wanted to do you harm (or you chasing them for the same reasons) with danger just centimeters from blowing you over. Living the LaVida Loca every waking moment.

She let herself think about her near misses in the past as she pulled off H-1, and down into the clogged streets. Her closest brush with death was a thief in Marseille. She had him cornered in a waterfront hotel room during an FBI on-the-job training mission. O.J.T.'s were a necessary part of the course, giving instructors the chance to observe *first-hand* a student's reaction in *real-time*. In Marseille, she lived because she fired first. Another split second, and it would have been her on the filthy bed…in a pool of her own blood. Then there was the night in Paris when fellow agent (and her fiancé), Jim Cooper, was killed. An FBI covert training mission to kidnap a high ranking Islamic terrorist fell apart, and she and Cooper were left behind, and tried to shoot their way out of the mess. Jim was shot in the chest seconds before a recovery force scooped them up and whisked them off to safety. Jimmy died in her arms on the way to the airplane that would fly them out of France. Her decision to move to the West Coast was her way of letting the ghosts of the past go and starting fresh in a new location and on her own. Now, if she shot someone, it would be on her—and not at the bidding of some bureaucrat or spineless corporate fat cat.

A blaring horn snapped her back from her reflections. A quick stop for gas and directions to Tuttle's street took less than ten minutes. While at the station, she paid a dollar and a half for a large cup of ice, wrapped a few chunks in a paper towel, and held it to her still-swollen face as she pulled away. Five minutes later, she found the street she was looking for, turned left, and shifted into park.

She sat, listening to the sounds of the neighborhood, letting the background noise alert her to anything unusual or out of place. During the daytime, neighborhoods sounded the same around the world, dogs barking, children playing, wives visiting, and a mechanical bustle from traffic nearby. Pearl City was no different than suburban L.A. or Detroit; everything sounded normal.

She was two blocks from Tuttle's place and was deciding whether to do a slow drive-by or walk it, when she spotted Wesley sitting in the pickup a half-block ahead of her. She hit the ignition and stomped the gas. The Vette seemed to leap the short distance as she slammed the brakes, skidded to a stop, and jumped out.

"Wesley Wagner Barrett, what the hell are you doing here?" Briar was mad. "You're supposed to be at the hotel."

"Yeah, and you're supposed to be at the airport," he said smugly. "I knew what you were up to when you threw so much *angel this, and honey that crap* at me. You may be four days older than I am, but you'll never outfox this Barrett-Man. Now, jump in and let's do a drive-by."

"Why I try so hard to protect your ungrateful little ass, I'll never understand," she snarled and punched his shoulder. "That's it, no more! You're on your own, buster; just leave me all that money you inherited, and we'll call it even."

"So, you are jealous that I'm rich and you're not. I knew it; I just knew it! You don't love me, you love my money. Ha! Auntie always said to watch out for the little redheaded bitch, she's after our money..." That was a lie, of course, but Wesley enjoyed taunting.

"Wesley, you'd better shut up. I'm in no mood for your bullshit. I know what you're trying to do, and it won't work. Maybe twenty years ago, but not now. You say one more mean thing to me, and I'll slap the snot out of you."

"Okay, okay, calm down, no need for violence. Let's save our strength for gecko-man..."

Briar swung her head and grabbed Wesley's arm. "What did you just call Tuttle? Was it gecko-man? Did you call him that because of the blood image on the bathroom wall?"

“No – because Porter told me that Tuttle has a giant tattoo of a gecko, running from his butt crack up over his shoulder and stopping just above his pelvic bone. He said that Tuttle would make him rub the gecko with warm oil until it gleamed. Porter was terrified at having to do it; he said Tuttle would almost go into a trance.”

“Detective Kanoa needs to know about this. I should call him now. This is getting more bizarre by the moment.”

“You’re not calling him yet, Briar. I want first shot at Tuttle. I’m not backing off now, so sit back and get a grip, tough girl!”

Wesley slowed as they approached the address. Briar edged down in her seat until only her eyes were visible, and of course her red hair. The front yard was nothing more than crushed coral with battered trash cans filled with garbage and litter strewn about. A motorcycle leaned on its kickstand in the shade of a coconut palm, as several scrawny cats batted at each other playfully.

The one window facing the small yard was covered with dark blue cloth (probably a sheet). The screen door was off its hinges and leaning against the window, further blocking the view, either in or out, Briar noted.

"Pull ahead to the corner and let me out; I want to take a look at the back of the place," she said. She pulled the automatic pistol out of the side pocket of her cross-body bag and ratcheted the slide back enough to confirm a round was seated in the chamber. She released the slide, as it slammed home.

"No way, Briar, leave that here; you'll just get yourself killed if you try to arrest him."

"Arrest him, are you crazy? I'm going to shoot him if he comes after me. Don't worry; I know what I'm doing."

"Oh, excuse me; I forgot for a minute that you were a regular Charlie's Angel back in the day," he said sarcastically.

"You're pissing me off again. Stop it while you still have your little nuts. Trust me; I have the situation under control."

Briar slid out of the cab and disappeared down a driveway, several houses down from Tuttle's hovel. She was gone less than thirty seconds when she reappeared, sprinting down the drive with a huge Pit Bull three strides behind her, stringy drool flying as he snapped powerful jaws inches from Briar's butt.

"Open the frigging door, Wesley," she screamed, as her arms pumped for speed, and her feet appeared to not even touch the ground…a cloud of coral dust billowing behind her and the crazed dog.

She didn't wait for an answer and dove through the open window, losing one of her new sandals in the leap. Wesley jammed the truck into gear and popped the clutch. The dog slammed into the side door and spun away. Wes had the truck up to forty within a half-block, with the dog running neck and neck, eyeing Briar as he ran alongside.

"Go faster...Cujo is keeping up with us, for Christ's sake. Look at him...he wants to kill us. *Local boys and their damned inbred fight dogs*...get us the hell out of here," Briar fumed.

Sometimes, Wesley was a little schitzo-nuttzo and did things for fun. This was one of those times. He slowed down and stopped, as he rolled down his window, and called out, "Here doggy, doggy, here boy, come to Mama."

Wrong thing to do. The massive dog didn't hesitate; taking a running leap and landing in the bed of the truck. Then he jumped onto the cab roof, and slid head-first down through the driver's side window before Wesley could roll it up. In less than a micro second, Briar and Wesley exited the truck via the passenger side, and shimmied up the nearest Banyan tree.

"Now's the time to use the gun, Briar. Shoot the fucker; he probably knows how to climb too."

It became a standoff. The mutt sat in the truck cab, slobbering all over the interior, while Briar and Wesley watched from the tree. With the passenger door wide open, she could see the dog's head buried in her open tote bag, scavenging for whatever. The big head came out with a bag of taro chips hanging from its jowls, and quickly wolfed it down, wrapper and all, then hastily made another dive into the bag.

"That was brilliant, Wesley, just brilliant. What the hell were you thinking? That dog is a trained killer, and definitely wants to kill us—so you pull an asinine stunt like that."

"Look at the positive side, Bri, when was the last time you climbed a tree, hmm?"

Briar shook her head in defeat, and then cracked a small smile. Wesley smiled back sheepishly, and soon the two were laughing at their predicament.

"Look at us, sitting in a frigging tree while a Pit Bull rummages through our vehicle. We've done crazy things together, but this…"

"Why you malihinis in my Banyan?" a big Samoan woman wearing a short muumuu that looked more like a tent, shouted at them, as she waddled across her yard. "Mo bettah you go back to Waikiki."

"We would like to get down, but we can't. There seems to be a rabid dog in the cab of our truck," Briar called down.

"What dog?" the woman asked, as she approached the truck. "Shoots, Sheila wouldn't hurt a fly."

The woman lumbered over and motioned for Sheila to get out. "Go home, you worthless *poi* dog, or *Tutu* take a cane to you."

Sheila glanced back over her shoulder as she trotted towards home, stopping to water the crushed coral en route, then off again, stub of a tail wagging.

Briar and Wesley looked at each other and broke out laughing again.

"What the hell?" Wesley said.

"Sheila must have been after the granola bars all along."

"I say we sit up here for a while, just to make sure that it isn't some of our fine *haole 'okole* she wanted, and not the granola bars," Wesley squinted his eyes against the late afternoon sun. "We can watch the front of Tuttle's house from here too."

A chirping came from the truck cab.

"That's my phone; I need to get it. The only people that know that number are Detective Kanoa and Auntie Dearest."

Briar picked her way down as quickly as she thought prudent, and then dropped the last six feet. Looking out for a flash of fur to come tearing up the street again, she hot-footed it to the truck and jumped in.

"Hello," she said.

"Briar, what took so long to answer, honey? Is this a bad time to talk?" Auntie Cyd's voice sounded far away.

This isn't good. She's probably at the airport waiting for me to pick her up. What should I say...? "Hi, Auntie, have you landed? I wasn't expecting you for another hour." Briar's mind was processing plausible lies, a dozen a second. "I can be there in thirty minutes, or better yet...why don't you and old what's his name take a taxi to the Royal? Wesley and I can meet..."

"Change in plans, Bri, and between us—I'm not too happy about it."

"What are you talking about, what kind of change in plans?"

"Arturo insisted that his mother attend the wedding, and that she come with us to Honolulu. He said that she won't 'fly commercial' anymore, because of some silly scare she had in Athens a few years ago. Apparently, there was a bomb threat on her flight."

"I can understand that. Who wouldn't be scared if they thought they might be blown out of the air by terrorists?"

"Of course, I understand, but that's not the issue. Arturo's mother Cecelia lives in Monterrey. So now I'm cooling my Jimmy Choos here in Mexico, as we've waited more than three hours for Mamasita and her entourage to arrive. Punctuality must not be part of her DNA."

Briar went limp with relief, mumbling under her breath, "God, there really is someone up there listening to my prayers."

"What's that about prayers, honey?"

"I was just thinking out loud—I said chairs…I should have ordered extra folding chairs."

"My poor Bri—playing wedding planner for your Auntie Cyd. I couldn't love you more if you were my own daughter. You were always such a bright and beautiful child—a perfect clone of me. Of course, there are those icky biological genes in there too—but nothing that my influence, a little makeup, and some minor plastic surgery can't fix…when the time comes, of course."

Aunt Cyd, always with the backhanded compliments, "This is really not a good time to go into all that. We know very little about my bio parents, so let's just pretend I got my bizarre genetics and characteristics by osmosis, from yours and Mom's side of the family."

"Briar, don't be impertinent; I'm under enough stress with this whole Arturo thing. I can't deal with hostility from you at the moment."

"Oh, Auntie, I'm not trying to make things hard for you. I fully understand your predicament (I guess). I am relieved to hear that you're safe and in Mexico. However, it sounds like you might be having second thoughts about marrying Arturo?"

"Don't scold me, Bri, but I think I possibly might be. With him insisting we detour to pick up his mother, a trickle of doubt played in the back of my mind. Then, when he casually dropped the bomb that she would be living with us a few months out of the year, I nearly fainted."

"Are you saying the wedding is off?"

"If his rude bitch-mama isn't aboard within fifteen minutes, I'm booting Arturo's fine ass off this Citation, and instructing the pilot (who's no slouch himself) to turn around and take me home."

"Home?"

"Yes, home to Kansas City. I'll teach that Mama's boy to blindside me," she sobbed.

"Don't cry, Auntie, everything is going to be fine. Do whatever is right for you. Wesley and I are behind you, no matter what," Briar said, as she wiped a tear of relief from the corner of her eye.

"I know you are, honey; I shouldn't have acted so fast. I need time to think this through; a few days back home on the Plaza will clear my mind. My girlfriends are there to console me, too," she said confidently. "Briar, I must go speak with Arturo before *Mother* arrives. This is just all wrong. Love to Angel. See that he stays out of trouble. I'll call you in a few days. Ta." Click. "Ta to you too, Auntie," Briar said, as the phone went dead in her hand.

Wesley was hanging on the door, listening to the conversation, and grinning broadly.

"Are we off the hook?"

"Yep, she's in Monterrey, Mexico with Arturo—getting ready to give him the old heave-ho."

"Poor guy, he doesn't know it yet—but even breaking up with our Aunt Cyd will cost him," he laughed.

Chapter 21

Kimo was exhausted; he hadn't slept more than a few hours since Senator Stanton's murder, and he was ready to collapse. Mano had dropped him off a half-hour earlier, and he was just stepping out of the shower when his cell phone pinged. Caller I.D. pegged it as Special Agent Thomson. He let it ring until it stopped, then began to towel himself off. A moment later, it rang again.

"Yes, Agent Thomson, what can I help you with?" he said irritably.

"Kanoa, why didn't you pick up when I called a moment ago? You're not being a team player, little man."

"Thompson, you ever call me *little man* again, I'll kick your *haole* rear end all the way back to Butt Crack, Texas or wherever your racist ass is from." Kimo was mad; he'd had enough of this prima donna, and wasn't going to take it.

"Whoa right there, Don Ho. Watch your mouth or I'll have your Internal Affairs people up your ass for insubordination," Thompson shot back. "Now, get your butt down here now. While you were out chasing rainbows, I arrested Stanton's murderer. I want you down here to help with the interrogation."

Kimo was surprised at this turn of events. There was no way Thompson had the right suspect.

"Give me some details about the arrest," he said.

"The only thing you need to know, Kimo-sabi, is that he was under your nose the whole time, and you didn't suspect him."

"Who did you arrest, Thompson?"

"Your pal from the Big Island, Jimmy Hinoko and his brother," Thomson chuckled. "Surprised, Detective?"

Kimo was shocked; this man is out of control.

"I'll be right down," he said and punched off, then hit Lieutenant Ping Lee's number.

"Lieutenant, Kanoa here. What the hell is going on? I just talked with our FBI friend, and he says they've arrested Jimmy Hinoko for the Stanton murder."

"Kimo, you better get down here stat. Jimmy's lawyers are threatening to sue the city, The TV people are outside, demanding to know what we have on Jimmy, and the mayor is nowhere to be found."

The phone went dead in his hand; he tossed it on his easy chair and cursed, then picked it back up and called the crime lab.

"HPD, Crime Lab, how may I help you?"

"Uncle, it's Kimo."

"I was hoping you would call. I have the report back from the National Laboratory."

"Tell me what we have," Kimo said excitedly.

"You need to read the data for yourself, Kimo. We indeed have a very dangerous man on our hands. The top line is that he is wanted on suspicion of murder in four states and a federal beef for manslaughter and arson."

"Arson? How does that fit in with his murder charges?"

"Says here that he burned a house down to cover a multiple murder. Once the fire was out, they found three charred bodies, all male, all dismembered."

"Okay, keep this to yourself until I get there."

He decided to walk the ten blocks from his small apartment to headquarters. A storm was moving in from the south with torrential rains soaking the city, making everything shiny and new. Lightning flashed in brilliant megaton explosions across the sky that squinted the eye and hunched sunburned shoulders protectively. Palm fronds waved in the wind, as food wrappers and trash from a million visitors danced down the deserted streets in turmoil. Kimo loved it.

"Howzit Kimo? Slip those shoes off," Uncle called out, as Kimo tossed his rain poncho in a heap by the door and shook his mop of wet hair. "We can't have you tracking up the place with those giant muddy shoes of yours."

Kimo was self-conscious about his big feet; he wore a twelve double E and his bare feet looked more like paddles with toes, which should have been on a much larger body.

"Don't make fun of my feet, or I might put one up your '*okole.*"

Uncle laughed and motioned Kimo to follow.

"This is a very bad man you are hunting, Kimo. Once his DNA hit a match on the national sex offender hot list, the computers went crazy, according to the operators. Indeed I have already had three calls from the mainland; one department is sending their serial killer expert to help locate Mr. Tuttle."

"Is that his name, Tuttle?" Kimo said, as he scribbled in his notebook. Jeremy Tuttle was the name Briar had given him too.

"Jeremy Tuttle is our man. He's gone by other names in other places, but Tuttle is his surname. Records show he spent twenty years in the Navy, mostly with the Pacific Fleet. Navy C.I.D. is searching their data banks for any open homicides that have the same M.O. as our boy's."

"What's his body count?"

"Well, the three I told you about found burned and quartered. Oregon has him at two for sure, three maybes. Houston has him down for his mother…"

"He killed his mother?"

"Yep, according to the Houston P.D, he beat her to death with a broom stick and left her where she fell. By the time they discovered her body, he was in the wind."

"Okay, that brings our boy to six and climbing on the mainland, then you add our four - gives us a running count of…ten…"

"Kimo, I am so proud of you. You didn't need to use your fingers to come up with the number," Uncle teased. "I think, though, that by the time we catch this *moke*, you'll need all your fingers indeed…and those nasty toes too."

Kimo entered the crowded conference room and flipped the fat manila folder on the tabletop, landing it squarely in front of the captain.

"Here's your killer, Captain," he said, ignoring Agent Thompson.

"What are you talking about, Kanoa? Our man is right through that door," Thompson said. "Like I said on the phone, while you're out chasing your tail, I got the job done."

Kimo continued to ignore Thompson and spoke directly to his commanding officer.

"The suspect's name is Jeremy Tuttle; last known address is in Pearl City. Occupation, while in the Navy, was as a cook-baker. Shouldn't be too difficult to run him down. We put some people on it, to hit all the hotels and resorts, and we'll flush him out."

"You people better start listening to what I'm saying here. I have our murder suspect right on the other side of that wall, and I'm taking him to D.C. with me tonight. He'll be arraigned tomorrow on accessory to murder charges, nice and tight. He did it, and if my guess is right, he's about to tell us who his muscle is…"

A loud thud rattled the glass partition of the interrogation room.

"What the hell are you guys doing in there?" Kimo said, as he hurried to the door just as it swung open and Jimmy Hinoko rolled out unconscious, blood beginning to spread from his broken nose.

Captain Lee was on his feet, "What the fuck do you think you're doing, Thompson? We don't beat suspects, for God's sake, man."

"Chill out, Lee, we're good. It's our word against the pineapple's here…"

"*Pineapple*! Why, you arrogant son of a bitch," Captain Lee went ballistic, pulled his sap off his belt, and smacked Thompson across the jaw. Thompson hit the floor next to Jimmy Hinoko and a trickle of blood dribbled out of his nose.

"Mano, cuff this '*okole puka*, and get a couple of jailers up here. Toss him in a holding cell."

Kimo stood and grabbed the FBI interrogator as he emerged from the small room. The agent was rolling up his sleeves and didn't see the fist coming at him from out of nowhere. The punch landed and he staggered back. Kimo moved in with a quick kick and the bigger man went down in a heap of pain.

"Put this *hupo* in the tank with Thompson," Kimo called over his shoulder, as he entered the interrogation room. The third agent was backed against the wall with his hands in the air, "Hey, be cool, man. I'm not looking for a beef with you."

Kimo kicked a folding chair out of the way, grabbed the agent by the shirtfront, and yanked him across the small table.

"Mano, take this one too; put him in with the *mahús*. He'll be screaming for mercy by morning."

Jimmy Hinoko was placed on a gurney and was being rolled down to the infirmary, when an AP stringer and his cameraman spotted the entourage. "Is that who I think it is?" The reporter yelled, turned to his cameraman, and shouted, "Chang, get this on live feed; that's candidate Jimmy Hinoko."

Camera lights flashed, blinding the orderlies momentarily. Within seconds, there were more cameras, more lights, and questions shouted from reporters rapidly filling the hallway.

Captain Lee, Mano, and Kimo pulled up short as they turned a corner and saw the disaster unfolding ahead of them.

"Oh, hell, we're screwed now. This will be flashed clear across the mainland…"

"Hold on, Skipper," Kimo said. "I have an idea. You stay here…Mano, you come with me." Kimo ran back to the conference room, where Thompson was sitting trying to clear his head.

Everyone grab an arm, and let's walk these douche bags down to the infirmary…when we hit the cameras, let's put on a show. If they want to see who beat up Jimmy, then let's show them."

A couple of minutes later, the three FBI men were frog-marched past the cameras by their jailers, for all the country to see.

Kimo stopped long enough to give a few words off the cuff, lapsing easily into "pidgin" for effect.

"Deez tree *cockaroaches*—dey beat up Jimmy Hinoko. Dis is Hawaii, not Gitmo…we don' beat on *bruddahs* here."

"What's your name, Sir?" a reporter called out.

"My name is Detective Kimo Kanoa. You can tell all deez *haoles*, when dey come to Hawaii, dey show respect for our people and our laws, or dey go to da poke just like deez FBI men, laying the *pidgin* on heavy. We don't care who dey are—and I speak for da Honolulu Police Department and da Mayor…"

Captain Lee grabbed Kimo's sleeve and pulled. "That's enough, Kimo, next thing you'll be announcing your candidacy for Stanton's seat." Kimo swaggered through the swinging doors, closing out all the shouted questions, and laughed.

"There won't be any blowback on us now, Captain. The world's going to know that it was the FBI who beat an innocent man while in custody."

"Kimo, what if Thompson was right about Jimmy Hinoko being behind Stanton's murder?" Mano asked sheepishly.

"Then, *brah*, we are definitely screwed."

Chapter 22

With the windows rolled up, the truck cab became unbearable. Briar fidgeted, trying to find a comfortable spot; her undies were wadded up in a tight "wedgie" that she couldn't free without pulling down her pants. She had to pee again, but didn't want to get further soaked from the downpour. An hour ago, when the heavens first opened, she had just squatted her bare bum behind a wall of bougainvillea. She made a hop-skipping dash for the truck, but was soaked by the time she slammed the door behind her.

"Sit on your heel, dammit, Briar," she remembered her mother Donna yelling at her as a little girl. Riding long distances in the car with mommy dearest, Briar always had to pee. Sitting on her heel actually worked, but she couldn't do it driving a truck with a standard transmission. The foot she'd normally sit on had to be free for the clutch. She'd just hold it a while longer, maybe the rain would let up before her bladder popped.

Briar wasn't a complainer, but she was pretty miserable. Besides being in pain from the beat-down she'd endured, she was hungry (Sheila the Pitt Bull had eaten her stash of goodies), and she needed a shower after her footrace with the dog and their tree climbing debacle. Now, she was soggy to the core, had been fighting off Pearl City mosquitoes for the last three hours, and desperately had to go *shi`shi*. What the heck—she should just pee in the truck cab—it already stunk so badly, a little piss couldn't make it any worse.

She hadn't seen the big Samoan lady again, or anyone else other than a couple small girls skipping rope earlier. The neighborhood was quiet. Wesley was off on a snoop-n-poop mission, as he called it, while she concentrated on the front of Tuttle's house. After the relief of Auntie Cyd's call about cancelling the wedding, they decided to sit on Tuttle. She was tempted to give Detective Kanoa a heads-up, but she wanted to wait just a bit longer.

Briar spotted a discarded beverage cup tossed behind the passenger seat, which she quickly retrieved, and had slid her pants down far enough to pee in the cup, when the cab door flew open and Wesley jumped in.

"He's rolling, start this thing up, and let's tail him," Wesley said excitedly. "See where he goes."

"Christ sake, Wesley, you scared the piss out of me. Don't just come jumping in like that; I could have shot you."

"Or pissed on me is probably more like it," Wesley scoffed, "Duck down now; here he comes."

The motorcycle's rumble was muted by the rain pounding on the cab roof, but his passing headlight shimmied on bright, and lit up the cab. As soon as Tuttle passed, Briar put the truck into gear and made a slow U-turn—allowing a little distance to open between them.

"Briar, I was scared to death; I was so close to Tuttle I could have touched him as he came out of his house. If he had glanced over by the window where I was crouched, he would have seen me, and I would be kibbles and bits for Sheila and her canine friends by now."

"What were you doing getting that close, Wesley? You told me you were going to scout out the neighborhood. You didn't say you were going peeping on Tuttle," she said, as she poked him in the ribs. "Wesley, what we have here is a failure to communicate. As the senior member of this stakeout, I insist that you level with me from here on out. Got that, buster?"

Briar's extreme discomfort had her on edge, and she was in no mood for Wesley's sarcasm, as (still unrelieved) she zipped up her pants and continued the slow chase.

"We will follow him to see where he goes; once we know, I'm calling Detective Kanoa, and we are bowing out."

"So, we're letting him get away with what he did to Porter and to you? Look at you, Briar, you'll need surgery to straighten your nose…and your eyes, who knows? Maybe they're permanently damaged."

"Let me worry about my looks; you just sit there and keep your eyes on Tuttle. I don't want to lose him in this rain."

Briar was ten car-lengths behind the speeding motorcycle as they sped west on the H-1. The motorcycle was kicking up a rooster tail of water as Tuttle swerved through and around traffic. Briar was keeping up, but barely. She thought she'd lost him, but then spotted brake lights as they lit up at the Waimalu off-ramp. She swerved over to the slow lane and eased down the ramp as Tuttle made a right towards the beach.

"Eyes sharp, I don't want to lose this *paniolo* now," she said, as she craned her neck for a better look.

The truck's wipers had seen better days and left streaks as they screeched loudly back and forth.

"Damn it, Briar, step on it…we're losing him." Wesley pounded the dash in irritation.

Suddenly, Tuttle was gone. They lost him.

"*The Fuck*!" Wesley screamed.

"Chill out; we'll find him."

At the next intersection, Briar spotted a single tail light two blocks down. She spun the wheel left, bounced over the curb, and boosted her speed. A block from where the taillights disappeared, she slowed.

"Fort DeRussy? What the heck is he doing here?"

"Do you see him?" she said, straining to see through the dark and rain.

"No, I don't see…wait a minute; there's his motorcycle. Pull over…pull over."

Wesley jumped out of the cab and ran to the cycle. It was Tuttle's, no doubt. He motioned for Briar to hurry, turned, and disappeared down a path.

“Wesley! Damn it. Wesley, wait for me,” Briar stage whispered. She kicked off her one remaining shoe (Sheila had probably devoured the lost one by now anyway) and slid out of the cab in her bare feet, grabbing her pistol before she began to run. The path was dark and spooky with the rain and heavy humidity creating a wispy layer of fog close to the ground. Briar looked over her shoulder every few steps to see if a zombie or Tuttle might be following her.

The air under the palm canopy was heavy with the sweet smell of tropical flowers and shrubs. Briar breathed through her mouth to avoid the sickening richness, which allowed her to hear better too. She was lost. Fort DeRussy had always been a confusing layout for her. As a teenager, she and her friends would lie on the beach there and flirt with all the servicemen that weren't shy about what they had in mind for the girls. Fort DeRussy was the place where she'd had her first drink straight out of a liquor bottle and had kissed a boy with her mouth open. She was thirteen at the time, but passed for eighteen.

Briar strained to hear voices or footsteps…anything. She knew vaguely that the beach was off to her right, only because of the deeper rumble of the surf rolling in.

"Wesley," she whispered loudly.

A hand reached out and covered her mouth; she struggled to get free, but the grip tightened.

"Shhh. Quiet, Tuttle is just over there," Wesley said, as he released his grip. "Hold my hand and keep quiet."

The rain masked their noise as they pushed through a grouping of Gardenia bushes. Wesley motioned for Briar to squat and remain still.

"...You said you would have the money, Your Honor." Tuttle had a grip on a much smaller man, and shook him as he spoke.

Briar gasped when she recognized the small, chubby guy, as the man that was with Kalani Stanton last night...or the night before. She was getting her days and times mixed up.

"These are the same as money. They're negotiable bonds; it's the same as cash, don't you understand?" the man pleaded.

"Shut the fuck up and let me think."

Tuttle had heard of bonds before, but didn't understand how they worked. Mayor Hilo wouldn't lie at this point; he understood that his life was hanging by a thread, and couldn't take the chance that Tuttle would snap his neck. Tuttle smiled at the thought, but before he killed him, he would introduce him to the gecko.

"All right, this is what I'm going to do. I'll keep these bonds and do the job, but now I want two hundred-thousand in cash by this time tomorrow. To make sure you don't rat me out, you'll be spending the night with me, and tomorrow we'll go to the bank together."

"You mean…you want me to go with you when you kill her?" Hilo clutched his chest and tried to break free from Tuttle's grip.

"That's right, Mr. Mayor. You can watch as I kill her, then we'll go to my place and have a little celebration…"

"I can't go with you…you're fucking crazy. I…I…uh, have to be at City Hall later tonight for a press conference. Our deal was that you would kill her if I gave you a hundred and fifty thousand dollars. There it is in your hand right now. We never agreed to more money, or that I would have to go with you…"

Briar was shocked at the conversation. She had to get to Mrs. Stanton before these two psychopaths arrived to kill her. She was doubly shocked that the little fat man was none other than the mayor of Honolulu.

She jerked on Wesley's shirt and motioned for him to join her.

They crept enough of a distance away that they couldn't be overheard.

"Wesley, you stay here and learn everything you can about their plan. I'll leave you the truck and grab a cab. I have to warn Craig's wife before they show up. On the way, I'll call Kimo and tell him to meet me at her place. Now, go back there, and call me as soon as they start for her house."

"Be careful, Bri, this man is bat-shit-crazy! Don't try anything dumb. Mayor Hilo is our man, Briar. He's the man behind Stanton's murder and now he's mopping up loose ends. Once he finds out you and I are on to Tuttle—we'll be on his hit list too. This is all starting to make sense to me. Now, get going, and text me when you get there."

Briar turned and ran as quickly as she could down the path that led to the beach. Once she reached the sand, she knew exactly where she was, and ran for the Sheraton Hotel. Hotel guests scrambled to get out of the running woman's way as she plowed through the outdoor restaurant and straight through the lobby. A taxi van was sitting waiting for a fare. She jumped in the back and yelled to the man, "I need to go to Kahala and fast, please!"

"I don't go to Kahala. I only do the airport run, Miss," the driver said listlessly. He tilted his head to see Briar in his review mirror as he spoke. The man was enormous. Briar pegged him for a Tongan.

"I said, I need to go to Kahala, now move it."

The driver rolled a toothpick from the right side of his big puckered lips to the left side. "Uh-uh, honey. We ain't going to Kahala…"

Briar stuck her pistol behind his right ear, and pushed.

"Kahala. Now."

"Yes, Ma'am. We're going to Kahala. Just take it easy with that gun. I got a wife and kids; we don't have much, but what we got it's paid for. We go to church every Sunday and Wednesday night. We're Witnesses and don't believe in violence…"

"Shut up and drive."

Twenty minutes later, Briar was pounding on the Stanton's front door.

"Mrs. Stanton, open up. It's an emergency, open up."

Briar stood back from the door and waited for a porch light to come on, or the door to open, but neither happened. She ran to the pool house, pulled the key from its hiding place where she'd left it a few nights ago, and hurried back to the front door. In an instant, she was inside and flipping on lights as she flew through the living room and into the hall leading to the bedrooms.

"Mrs. Stanton, are you home? Come on out. Don't be afraid; it's me, Briar Malone—you know, your husband's little whore."

Mrs. Stanton was spread out across the bed at an angle with her robe open, exposing her gorgeous body. Briar ran to her and bent over for a closer look; her worst fear was that she was dead and that she hadn't arrived in time. One whiff and she knew Kalani was alive. The woman was drunk. She reeked of alcohol. Briar backed off and stood with her hands on her hips.

"No wonder Craig screwed around. Who wants to have sex with a limp body? Never mind," Briar thought. "I guess that's a whole other subject."

"I need to be paid, Ma'am. Gun or not, I need my fare money," the van driver said as he stood in the doorway, eyes glued to Kalani's half-nude body.

"Is she going to be all right, Miss?"

"She will be once you get your *moke* ass out of here."

"Uh, yes, Ma'am. You owe me a hundred dollars, plus parking…"

"A hundred dollars! Plus parking! Are you crazy? That was a thirty-dollar ride, and we didn't park anywhere."

"That's what I get for a run out to the airport, so I got to charge you the same, or I won't make my nut."

Briar spotted Kalani's Louis Vuitton handbag and opened it. She took two crisp one hundred dollar bills out and folded them, "Here's your fare; I'll double it if you wait here with me until the police arrive."

"The police! Why they coming? She's only drunk. Give her a few hours and she'll be up and walking around."

"There are men coming here to kill her; I need you to stay with me until the police get here. You do that, and I'll triple your fare."

"That's all I have to do is just hang around? Yes, Ma'am, I can do that. Little Mikey Mymua ain't scared of nothing."

“Go move your van down the street and then come back. I'll turn off all the lights and we'll wait in the dark. Are you okay with all this, Mikey?”

Little Mikey's face split into a huge grin, one front tooth was missing. “*Sistah*, fo dat kine money, I'll whip Tyson.”

Briar was worried that she hadn’t heard from Wesley and poked around in her bag for her phone. After a moment, she held it wide to see down into the clutter. Then she remembered, she had left it on the front seat of the truck, grabbing her gun instead of her phone when she hurried after Wesley at DeRussy Park.

“You're getting sloppy, Malone,” she mumbled to herself, as she entered the kitchen and fished around for Detective Kanoa's card. She found it and punched the number into the phone sitting on the counter.

Kimo picked up on the first ring, “Detective Kanoa speaking—who’s this?”

“Kimo, it’s Briar Malone; we have a problem. Jeremy Tuttle is definitely our killer. I’ll give you all the details later. He’s on his way to Kalani Stanton’s house to kill her. He has Mayor Hilo with him. Hilo is the one behind the murders; I heard him myself no more than an hour ago talking about killing Mrs. Stanton…”

“Slow it down, Briar. You're talking too fast. You say that Tuttle is on his way to Kalani Stanton's house to kill her, and that Mayor Hilo is with him and is the person behind the murders?”

"Yes, yes—you heard correctly. I'm here at the Stanton house now; Mrs. Stanton is drunk and passed out. I need you to get here before Tuttle arrives…”

“Can you get her into your car and drive away? I'll get some patrol units there just as soon as I hang up…”

“You're not thinking, Detective. We need to be here when they arrive, so they can be arrested. I'm not going anywhere, and if you send the

Keystone Cops, Tuttle will run for the back country."

"Briar, I command you to get out of there now. I'll take over from here. I can't have a citizen, and especially a woman, in danger like this. You don't know half the story on our boy Tuttle."

"Cut the crap, Kimo. I know what I need to know about the bastard. I know he likes to stick broom handles up his victims' butts before he kills them. I know he has a badass tattoo that runs from his ass hole to his Johnson as some kind of crazy Freudian phallic symbol…and I have a pistol that I can shoot the son of a bitch with if he attacks me again. So, get your ass over here, and let's bring this psycho down."

Briar slammed the phone back into its cradle and stood drumming her fingers on the countertop nervously as she thought what the best way would be to protect Kalani. She pulled the refrigerator door open and leaned in; she was ravenous.

"Carrots? Is that all this woman eats, carrots?"

Briar stuck one of the carrot sticks in her mouth that she'd found in Kalani's huge Sub Zero refrigerator and crunched it as she dialed Wesley's number. The call had barely connected and Wesley was on the line.

"Where are you, Briar? You left your fucking cell phone in the damn truck," he said in a muffled voice. "We got it wrong, Briar. They weren't talking about Kalani Stanton; they were talking about Hilo's wife. Their plan is to kill Hilo's wife…like NOW!"

"But, I thought they were talking about Kalani. Dammit, I really screwed up. Are they still at the park?"

"No, I followed them to Waialae Iki Ridge; I'm hiding in Hilo's backyard by the pool. I can see Tuttle and Mrs. Hilo from where I am. He has her tied to a chair and is waving his arms at her and yelling something. Oh, my God, he just tore his shirt off, Briar. Porter was right about the tattoo. It looks…almost real. I'm scared shitless, Briar. It's time to call in the cops."

"Stay put and give me the address; I'll call Kimo back, and I'll get there as fast as I can. Is there anything you can do to help the woman?"

"I don't know. Hurry and get here; meanwhile, I'll think of something. I think he's working himself up into some kind of frenzy…just get the cops up here fast."

Briar scribbled the address on an envelope, then slammed the phone down. She tossed the carrot blunt into the sink and called out, "Mikey, change of plans. Bring the van around, then help me get Mrs. Stanton loaded. I can't leave her behind alone; too many strange things are going on."

"Where are we going, Ma'am," Little Mikey asked. "I'll need nut money if we're going any place other than back to the Sheraton."

“Don’t worry, Mikey,” Briar told him. “I’ll cover your damned nut!”

Chapter 23

The rain beat loudly on the glass-topped patio table as Wesley attempted to fit his body beneath it to avoid the downpour. It was a waste of time, really, since he was already drenched. He trembled from the dampness, in spite of the temperature being in the mid-eighties, as his teeth began to chatter. If truth were told, he knew that some of the trembling and chattering were because he was frightened. He knew inside that he was more a proponent of flight than of fight. However, in the past when the need arose, he'd always acquitted himself rather well, even if he said so himself. It just wasn't in his nature to seek out trouble, but this was different. A serial killer maniac was less than twenty yards away doing some kind of ritual dance around Mrs. Hilo, the mayor of Honolulu's wife. This was insane. If he just stayed in hiding until Briar arrived, he would be safe. No one could see him out here in the dark underneath the table. However, if he just waited…then Tuttle could easily kill the poor woman, while he did nothing but watch.

Wesley set his chin in resolve and crawled out from under the table. It was time to man-up. He wiped rain from his eyes and started for the sliding doors. He pulled up as he got closer. Mayor Hilo was blindfolded and tied to a chair, struggling against the bindings. Wesley backed into the shadows of a large potted palm, spread the fronds, and peeked through the wet glass.

Tuttle swung his enormous head toward the doors, leaning forward for a closer look. Wesley was faint with fear; had he been seen? The moment passed and Tuttle went back to Mrs. Hilo. Wesley let the air out of his lungs in a quiet whoosh.

"Close, but no cigar, Jeremy," Wesley whispered. "Another couple of steps, and I would have been forced to rip you apart."

He needed a weapon. Tuttle was just too powerful a man to take on barehanded. Wesley hurried over to the lava-stone grill and hunted through the cookout utensils for an equalizer. His hand wrapped around a long-handled fork.

“I’ll poke him a few times with this baby, and he’ll squeal like a *luau* pig,” he laughed mischievously, turning back toward the doors.

“Who the hell are you?” Tuttle was charging toward Wesley with hate smeared across his ugly face.

Wesley screeched and lunged forward…driving the fork into Tuttle’s abdomen. Tuttle stopped, looking down in shock at the protruding handle.

“Why, you little runt, you’re a dead man,” Tuttle bellowed, as he yanked the tines out of his gut.

Wesley didn’t bother hanging around to admire his handiwork. He made straight for the sliding door, hurtled through the narrow opening, and slid it shut. His shaking fingers found the latch and fumbled it locked. Mrs. Hilo’s muffled screams grew louder when she saw Wesley approaching, looking more like a ghoul than a liberator.

"It's okay; calm down," he said, and untied the knotted cloth from her mouth.

"Look out!" Mrs. Hilo screamed.

Her enormous terrified eyes froze Wesley to stone. A microsecond later, a patio chair crashed through the glass door. The shattered glass exploded into the room, covering Wesley and Mrs. Hilo. Another microsecond and Tuttle was on top of Wesley, grabbing him in a headlock and torqueing down hard on his neck. Wesley struggled to free himself from the monster's grip.

"Ya fuck! Ya spying fuck! You want a piece of this, huh?" Tuttle shouted, spraying foamy spittle as he yelled.

Mrs. Hilo tumbled over as she attempted to move away from the struggling men. Wesley's eyes felt huge as Tuttle squeezed tighter. He watched Mrs. Hilo crawl across the floor in an insane spasmodic scuttle. Her screams were shrill. Wesley's mind filled with dread as it flashed on a wounded animal caught in a leg trap, then the piercing sounds of pain (his own) snapped him back.

There was no way he was going to die like this, not with this big brute choking the life out of him. Briar's childhood admonishment to kick a bully in the nuts flashed across his oxygen-starved brain. With a burst of adrenalin, he reached between his spread legs, grabbed Tuttle's groin, and squeezed.

The reaction was instantaneous. Tuttle let go and stumbled back in agony. Wesley ran to Mrs. Hilo, grabbed her by a foot, and dragged her behind him as he ran through the dining room into the entryway. He caught a glimpse of Mayor Hilo's horrified eyes as he ran past him, but didn't slow down. He wanted to get Mrs. Hilo out of the house before Tuttle regained his focus.

The safety of the dark rainy night was just beyond the closed front door, when Tuttle landed on Wesley's back and pounded him with sledgehammer fists. Wesley fell into a protective ball, with his legs pulled tight to his chest and arms guarding his head. Wesley's nose exploded across his face in a starburst of pain, as he melted into blissful unconsciousness.

Tuttle stood over Wesley's body, breathing easily; the struggle of the last few minutes didn't seem to faze him. He glanced over at the screaming woman and kicked her in the head to shut her up.

"Hilo, I'm going to cut you loose to help me with these two lumps of meat. If you try anything funny, I'll kill you too."

Tuttle took Wesley's wallet and thumbed through the credit cards, keeping the major ones. When he saw Wesley's address on his driver's license, he sneered as he mumbled…"So, you're Porter's sugar daddy. Coming around looking for a little payback, bitch?" Tuttle lashed out with a vicious kick to Wesley's chest. "Did you think you were going to shut me down?" he said and kicked again. "You lose, bitch. Now I'm inviting you to MY party, Mr. Barrett. Too bad poor Porter can't make it, but you'll tell me where you're hiding him before we blow the candles out…won't you, bitch?"

Tuttle opened Wesley's cell and scrolled through the call list. Briar's name was listed at least a half dozen times from Wesley's panicked calls to update her.

"So the *ilio wahine* that stabbed me is working with you, huh, Mr. Sugar Daddy? I'll have to admit, you two are clever, picking up my scent, so to speak. Did you two find me in the yellow pages or did a little birdie named Porter tell all?"

Tuttle was moving around the kitchen as he talked. This was a trick that Dee used to noodle through situations beyond her limited intellect. She would backhand little Jeremy if he ever interrupted these one-sided discussions, "Shut up, you little bastard…you're just like that worthless excuse of a man father. Stop always interrupting me when I'm thinking!"

Tuttle stopped in the center of the kitchen. He had a perplexed look on his face as he gazed up at the ceiling. He appeared to be frightened, but then his fear turned into a snarling rage. He tore the hanging pot rack from the ceiling in a powerful yank. The metal pots and pans crashed to the floor in confusion. Tuttle snatched up a large frying pan and threw it at Mayor Hilo; it sailed across the room, striking Hilo in the head and knocking him unconscious.

"Great, just fucking great," Tuttle said. "Don't you be dead on me, Your Honor, not till I get my money, you cocksucker."

Tuttle leaned back on the sink, feeling weak. For the first time, he noticed the blood flowing from the fork wound. He spilled drawers open, searching for a dishcloth or napkin to plug up the wound. He shook out a couple of Handi-Wipes from a package and shuffled across to a mini-bar in the dining room. He hated booze. Only weak people needed booze to make them feel strong. Not Jeremy Tuttle. Jeremy didn't need anything except…Gecko.

He smacked the neck off a bottle of Jack Daniels on the edge of the table, leaving a sharp jagged edge, as he soaked the wipes with the smelly brown liquid. The burn of the alcohol on the wound gritted his teeth. As the burn tapered down, he poured liquid across the puncture wound on his upper back from last night's tussle with the redheaded bitch in the penthouse. He poured the last of it across his abdomen, letting it mix with his blood and flow to the floor. He stood staring at the pool of blood for a moment, then refocused.

"I have to get out of here before sweetmeat shows up with the Shore Patrol. Can't have that, can I? No brig time for this sailor. I'm weighing anchor for safer ports."

Tuttle found bed sheets in the laundry room to tie Wesley up with, then he untied Mrs. Hilo from the chair, and hogtied her with her arms and legs trussed up behind her.

"Try crawling now, ya fat pig." He laughed and gave her a good solid kick to the rump.

"Wake up, *brah*. I need you to help me get these two lumps out to the car."

Tuttle cut through the laundry room to the garage, and raised the heavy door effortlessly. He opened the four doors to the mayor's plain, unmarked sedan. Tuttle left his motorcycle at Fort DeRussy, once he had decided to keep the mayor with him. Using the mayor as a witness to his wife's murder was a stroke of genius. He would own the mayor completely, and would keep him alive for as long as it took to drain him dry of every worldly possession the fat fuck owned.

Tuttle stood in the garage, watching the rain clouds scud across the night sky. The lights from Honolulu glowed ghostly through the dense downpour. He would miss Hawaii, but it wasn't safe any longer. It was time to move on. He knew that he had lost control of Jeremy and was now more his mother Dee than anyone else. The burn that flowed from his mind to his…gecko was euphoric. He was in a constant state of mental tumescence, providing a feeling of invincibility. He loved himself, he loved what he had become, and what he did to satisfy the hunger.

He hurried back into the house and untied Hilo.

"Snap out of it, Hilo; we're getting out of here before the coconut cops show up and we have a shootout."

Mayor Hilo staggered to his feet, wiping the blood from the gash in his forehead, caused by the pan Tuttle had hurled at him.

"Where are we going? I need to call my service; I'm never supposed to be out of phone contact for more than an hour without checking in."

“Shut up and grab that little prick’s feet. Oh, I’m sorry, you two haven’t met, have you? Forgive my manners. Your Honor, meet Dead Boy…Dead Boy, meet Wife Killer.” Tuttle roared at his own joke. “Top that, Hilo; bet ya can’t.”

Hilo dropped Wesley twice as they maneuvered through the kitchen and laundry room. Wesley would wonder later where the cut on the back of his head came from, but for the moment, it was nothing. Tuttle picked Wesley’s limp body up easily and tossed him in the trunk of the sedan. A few minutes later, he tossed Mrs. Hilo alongside of Wesley.

“Okay, Coach, now you. Climb in.”

“I can’t fit in there,” Hilo said defiantly.

Tuttle slapped him across the face with an open palm. Hilo staggered back from the impact and whimpered.

“Get in, or I’ll cut an ear off.”

Hilo set his rump on the lip of the trunk and let himself fall back on top of his wife, trying to elbow his way in. It wasn't working; there just wasn't enough room. He continued to burrow down, using his elbows and legs as he witnessed the madness on Tuttle's face.

Tuttle slammed the trunk door down and leaned on it to close the last six inches. He could hear a muffled voice, but ignored it, and just kept pushing down. After a few bounces, the door snapped closed. He listened for any sound, but all was quiet.

He put the side of his head on the trunk, and began to sing his childhood prayer…

"Now I lay me down to sleep, I pray the Lord that Dee he keep…"

He moved away from the trunk, howling with laughter—as he danced a quick jig and jumped behind the wheel of the car, still singing…

"If I should die before I wake, I pray the Lord that Dee he take."

He tore down Laukahi Street, fishtailing onto Kalanianaole Highway—peals of laughter echoing into the night as he continued his song…

"If I should live for other days, I pray the Lord NOT to guide my ways."

Chapter 24

Little Mikey wiped at the foggy windshield with his hand, craning his neck as he drove up the winding street.

"Dis not good night be driving *Mauka* on Laukahi; she be dark, and *haoles*, dey don't number der yards," he complained.

"We have to be close, Mikey," Briar said, as she leaned forward behind the huge driver. "Just keep going. All the streets up here dead-end eventually. We'll turn around and look again, if need be."

"Where am I? Who are you people?" Kalani slurred drunkenly as she tried to sit up.

Briar swung around, just as Kalani slumped over and slid off the back row seat onto the floor. Briar shook her head in disgust and turned back toward the front.

“There it is, Mikey—pull over; that’s our truck,” she said, pounding Mikey’s shoulder. “Cut your lights; we’re close.”

Briar slid the side door back, tripped, and went to her knees, as she slipped on the wet running board. “It doesn’t hurt. It doesn’t hurt,” she said through clenched teeth, “Crap…that hurts!”

The truck was unlocked and smelled of dog. “Sheila, the mutt that keeps on giving…”

Briar gave a sigh of relief as she found the keys in the ignition; a moment later, she had her cell phone in her hand. She was surprised at the security she felt just having that small device back in her possession; it was her lifeline to Wesley and Kimo. She clutched the phone tightly to her chest as she rocked back and forth, letting the craziness of the last few days wash over her. She didn’t think she could take much more; when was it going to end? She didn’t even know if Wesley was alive. What if he was hurt, or worse—what if he was dead? The thought of Wesley dead splashed across her mind like battery acid…

"No frigging way," she said. "Briar, stop the pity party and get your rear in motion. Wesley needs you."

She strode back to the taxi-van and stuck her head in.

"Mikey, I want you to turn around and drive directly to HPD's main building on South Hotel. Tell them Briar Malone said for Detective Kanoa to pay you the fare…double it, whatever it is."

"But, what about you, Ma'am? I can't leave you out here alone."

Briar saw genuine sincerity in Mikey's face.

"I'm fine. My friend is up that driveway waiting for me; he'll protect me. I need you to leave before Mrs. Stanton wakes up again and causes a scene. Leave her at HPD; maybe they'll put her in the drunk-tank until she sobers up."

"They ain't going to do dat, Ma'am. Don't you know who she is? She's like royalty. The people love her and treat her like a queen. Those coconuts will wipe her '*okole* if she says, and even if she don't say."

"Whatever. Get your nut money and go home, Mikey. You did good tonight, real good."

Little Mikey turned a dark brown blush and lowered his eyes. Briar thought he looked like a little boy as she leaned in the window and gave him a peck on the cheek.

She waited until the van's taillights disappeared down the hill and started up the long driveway. Wesley had said he was in the backyard hiding, so she made her way to the edge of the yard farthest from the house, just to play it safe and not be seen. Briar found a Billabong ball cap in the truck, and pulled it down low over her eyes to divert the rain. She threaded her long red hair through the Velcro opening in the back of the cap, forming a frizzy, wet ponytail. Her thin white top clung to her damp breasts, revealing more than she preferred, but she couldn't be bothered under the circumstances.

The pool deck was a huge slab of embossed concrete with scattered potted flowers and small islands of palms, philodendron, and trellises of jasmine. Everything was wet and shiny from the falling rain. From her vantage point, she could see straight into the kitchen, dining room, and family room, but no Wesley. Her pulse kicked up a few notches as she got closer and saw the wreckage of the sliding door and a blood trail leading across the kitchen floor. She squeezed the pistol grip tighter and called out, "Wesley? Wesley, are you in there? Answer me if you can hear my voice."

The silence fed fear to her jangled nerves and she started to hyperventilate. She recognized the first signs of panic and slowed her breathing.

"Tuttle, where's my cousin, you crazy mother fucker?" she yelled out.

No answer. Knowing the house was empty was scarier than if it was filled with the dead. Her hand shook as she stepped cautiously through the shattered glass door. She studied the blood trail as it wound its way through the dining room, where there was an overturned chair with lengths of rope lying about. The blood continued into the foyer, where there was pooling blood, and then it doubled back to the kitchen.

She knew the place was empty, but she needed to be sure. She ran through the upstairs, checking all the rooms, turning on lights as she ran. Back downstairs, she followed a blood trail out to the garage, and then out onto the drive.

At least one person, maybe two, still alive. Her guess was that Tuttle and Mayor Hilo carried out their plan to kill Mrs. Hilo. Wesley tried to help, probably lost, and might also be dead. Tuttle and Hilo took the bodies somewhere else to dump them??? Briar sobbed out loud in anguish. Wesley couldn't be dead. She wouldn't stand for it. Please, God, don't let him be dead.

Again, she pulled herself back from the brink and blocked out the bad images. She crammed the pistol into her waistband and looked at her cell phone.

“Please answer, Angel,” she muttered, as she hit his speed dial.

Wesley's stupid chime sounded…once…twice…thre…

“I've been waiting for your call, sweetmeat.”

Briar jerked the cell away from her ear and stared wide-eyed at it. Oh, my God, it's Tuttle!

“Briar, this is you, isn’t it?” Tuttle asked with a chuckle.

“Yes, Tuttle, it’s Briar. Where’s my cousin?” she managed to ask.

“Oh, you must mean the soon-to-be-dead pretty boy? He’s here with me.”

“Is he…still…alive?” she asked in a shaky whisper.

“That depends on what you mean by alive. Is he breathing? …Yes. Will he be breathing much longer? …No. You might say he’s ‘dead boy breathing’.” Tuttle’s roar of laughter overloaded the cell’s volume, causing it to crackle and pop.

“Where are you now, Jeremy?” Briar asked, composing herself with great difficulty.

“Don’t you call me Jeremy! I didn’t say you could call me that,” he roared.

“Tell me where you are, Tuttle. I’d like to come visit you, maybe we can talk a little.”

“My name is Dee,” he hissed.

“Dee? Okay, Dee…how about I trade you me for Wesley? Just tell me where we can make the trade. I’m sure you and I can have a good time together…”

“SHUT UP and listen, *kola wahine*. I’ll show you good time. Oh yeah, a REAL good time. If I like what I get, maybe I think about letting dead boy live. I won't let him go, but I won't kill him either…unless he begs me to kill him."

Briar was frozen in fear; she tried to continue the conversation, but her mind couldn't formulate anything coherent.

"Sweetmeat, are you still there?"

"Yeah, I'm here, Dee."

"So, do we have a deal—you for pretty boy's life?"

"Tell me where you are; I'll come there now."

"You know where I am."

The cell went dead.

Chapter 25

Fear pecked at the folds of Briar's mind as she sped west on H-1 toward Pearl City. She zipped past slower cars in her frenzy to get to Wesley. Her mind was exploding with visions of his body ripped and bitten. Tuttle was insane; nothing would stop him from killing Wesley and her. He had nothing to lose. Her only chance to survive the coming encounter with *Dee* was to shoot him; don't give him a chance to get his hands on her. If she faltered, he would break her into little pieces. No, she would definitely go in shooting.

Her cell dinged, startling her, and making her jump. The truck swerved dangerously into the center lane.

"Briar, where the hell are you? I called the last number I talked to you from, and some *buggah* answered. What the hell is going on?" Kimo was upset.

Briar was relieved to hear the detective's voice, and started to blurt out all the happenings of the last hour, but then she stopped. If she told Kimo where she was, he might beat her to Tuttle's place in Pearl City. He and his cops could fumble things and get Wesley killed. No way could she allow that.

"I…I'm at Mayor Hilo's house, on Waialae Iki Ridge," she lied. "It's a crime scene; you better get up here. I…uh…I'm hiding in back by the pool."

"Bullshit! Briar, don't lie to me. A patrol car just radioed that a redhead was speeding in a pickup truck on H-1 towards Pearl City."

Briar checked her rearview mirror for any sign of a cop as she instinctively lightened up on the gas pedal.

"I don't see any cop…oops!" It was too late; she'd just confirmed that she was indeed on the H-1. Her escape and evasion skills were rusty; she'd have to work on that—providing she survived.

"Okay, Kimo, you got me. I'm on my way to Tuttle's house. He says he has Wesley, and I'm confident that he has the mayor and his wife too. The only sign of any of them at the Hilo house was blood-smeared floors and a trashed kitchen."

"We are pulling into the mayor's drive as we speak. Every light in the place is lit up. Is that you're doing?"

"Yeah, I did a quick sweep, looking for bodies; couldn't find any. My guess is that Tuttle got spooked when Wesley showed up, and moved on him."

"You think Wesley moved on Tuttle? I hope you're wrong. Our man Tuttle has slipped completely over the edge. We're treating him as the most dangerous man on the Island right now. We have people at the airport, the cruise docks, and the marinas…all on high alert, watching for him, with orders to take him down."

"You don't need to tell me he's gone totally cra-cra. I talked to him less than fifteen minutes ago. Kimo, I was terrified just listening to him on the phone. He says his name is Dee and not Jeremy any longer. He went crazy when I called him Jeremy. I don't know what the hell that means."

"Dee was his mother. He killed her in a psychotic rage. The shrinks have a name for whatever it is that is driving him. To me, he's just a fucking nutcase that we have to stop before he kills again."

"Well, I need to find Wesley and get him to safety before you and your boys do a Ruby Ridge thing on him."

"Briar, you're going to get yourself killed. You must back off; Tuttle won't hesitate to kill you…he's out of control."

Briar felt a freezing chill of fear run through her body.

"I have to go; my off ramp's coming up," she said, and hung up.

Five minutes later, she cut the engine and headlights, letting the truck roll silently up to Tuttle's yard. The tires crunching on the wet coral was the only sound. She let the clutch out slowly as the pickup bucked to a stop. It took her a moment to realize that the rain had stopped too. With the pistol locked in both hands, she crept to the front window and peeked inside. A nightlight from a backroom cast a ghostly glow—melting everything into odd shadowy shapes.

She made her way to the backyard, standing on tiptoes to peek over the kitchen windowsill. By lifting herself in a chin-up pull, she made out a narrow bed in another room…

Something brushed against her leg. Her mouth opened in a silent scream. She twisted around midair, raising her pistol at the same time. She dropped down in a shooter's two-handed stance, with her finger on the trigger—just a microsecond from popping a cap.

Sheila sat on her butt with her paw extended to be shook, tongue hanging from her toothy maw, and drool stringing down from both sides of it.

Briar exhaled, falling back hard against the door and sliding down…landing on her butt.

"Sheila, damn it," Briar whispered. "You scared the crap out of me!"

Sheila scooted forward on her haunches, not bothering to stand, licking Briar's hand.

"You silly bitch. If I didn't hate you so much, I'd lick you back. This is the second time today that you've given me a heart attack," she said, as she quickly scratched Sheila's broad head.

Seeing her opening, Sheila moved in as close as she could to Briar and sat in her lap as she began licking her face.

"Get off of me, you big hairball; I'm not here to play kissy face with the neighborhood's security system," she said, as she tried to shoo away her new best friend.

"Go home. I'm kinda in the middle of a situation here, and you're gonna get me killed…"

Briar rummaged through her canvas bag, still hanging faithfully across her body…finding a flattened bag of nuts from the plane. She ripped the package open with her teeth and tossed it against the back fence. Sheila was on it in a single bound, swallowing (paper and all) as she turned back to see her new buddy disappearing around the corner of the house and into the truck.

Briar was stumped. How did she arrive sooner than Tuttle? Her fingers drummed the dashboard. Off in the distance, sirens wailed…lots of sirens. "Here comes the fuzz. Another two or three minutes, and the place will be lit up like Chinese New Year…"

Briar shot up straight, smacking her forehead with the palm of her hand.

"Tuttle, you sneaky son of a bitch!"

She ground the starter till the pickup's engine kicked in, then floored the gas pedal. She turned at the end of the block, just as the first two cop cars fishtailed around the other end of the street. She hit the H-1 on-ramp just as a string of emergency vehicles with flashing lights and sirens wailing roared down the off-ramp on the other side.

Chapter 26

It was a quarter to three in the morning when Briar pulled down the garage ramp beneath the penthouse high-rise. The sudden quiet from the rain hitting the truck's roof was immediately noticeable. Her thoughts had screamed to be heard over the roar of rain hitting the metal roof as she raced across Honolulu from Pearl City. Now, she had to consciously ratchet back the volume to a whisper. The spookiness of the garage had always bothered her, even in daylight…but tonight, it was worse. The pools of light every fourth or fifth stall added to the eeriness. Unexplained geometric shadows angled off in surreal patterns, and the smell was disgusting. It was a damp mix of ancient urine, motor oil, and mildew. The perfect stalking grounds for four-legged and two-legged vermin. She double-timed across the garage, swiveling her head as she ran. Once in the lobby, she took a moment to collect herself and steady her nerves. Once in the elevator, there was no turning back.

She checked the round in the chamber of her pistol, letting the slide slam home. "That *snikking* sound is becoming an all too familiar one," she mused, as she dug for her canister of pepper spray. She pulled her bag up over her head and stashed it behind a big potted fern, glanced down at her bare feet, and sighed tiredly. She caught a glimpse of herself in the floor-to-ceiling mirror on the far wall of the elevator lobby and made a face. She didn't recognize herself; she looked like a second cousin to Sheila, with her swollen eyes and jaw; her lips were unnaturally puffy too, from one of the poundings—which one, she couldn't recall. Add a little drool and she could easily pass for a Pit Bull. She pulled the cap off and shook her long hair back and forth, leaning forward and quickly knotting it up as she pulled the cap back on with the bill facing backward. She was ready.

The elevator ride seemed an eternity, but then, all too soon, the door whispered open. Briar knew immediately that her hunch was correct. The foyer lights were out, the penthouse door stood ajar, and there was a sharp smell of something rotten.

Her body jerked in fear when the *bing-bing* of her cell rang out. She dropped the can of pepper spray when she grabbed for the phone. The canister rolled off into the dark.

"Yes," she whispered.

"Oh, you're a smart one, sweetmeat," Tuttle's voice whispered back. "You drove all the way to Pearl City before you realized where we would be."

"Where is Wesley?" she said in a forced calm voice.

"Dead boy? He's still here with me. Sleeping right now, but I can wake him if you like."

"I'd like."

Briar tiptoed to the front door and quickly sidestepped through it, slamming the door behind her.

She flinched and screamed at the horrific howl of pain that came from the master bedroom. She recognized that howl. She would know that howl from anywhere on earth.

“Wesley, I’m here. You’ll be okay now.”

Another scream of anguish echoed through the walls.

“Tuttle, you bastard, stop it,” Briar yelled, waiting to hear from where the answer would come.

She leaned forward, trying to hear the slightest sound of movement from Aunt Cyd’s bedroom. She tiptoed down the hallway. A sound from behind froze her in place. The hair on her neck tingled; someone was behind her…she could feel a presence. She dare not look back, her body was trembling, and she breathed shallow breaths through her mouth. She wanted to run, scream, puke, pee…but she forged ahead.

“Welcome to Lego Land, Briar Malone,” a woman’s voice said softly, directly behind her.

Briar jumped, but didn't look behind her as she lurched for the master bedroom. She crashed the door open and slammed it behind her, gulping air. She screamed again when she saw Wesley tied spread-eagle to the far wall. His arms were spread wide and tied to stud-attached wall sconces. One leg was tied to the foot of an armoire, the other hung at a strange angle. Mayor Hilo stood to the side of Wesley, holding a small lighter fluid canister used for lighting the fireplace. Wesley's abdomen and legs were black from burns. Dozens of bruised and bleeding bite marks covered his shoulders and neck. Blood poured from a wound on his chest, running down across his abdomen, and on to the Moroccan tiled floor.

Briar was horrified; she stood straight and walked towards Hilo, pointing the pistol at his head. She felt she might be going insane.

"Did you do this?" she demanded. Her voice was shaky, and she didn't recognize it. "Did you, Mayor?"

“Smith, or whatever his name is, killed Margo and threatened to kill me too if I didn't help him with dead boy here.” Hilo began to sob. “He killed Margo with his bare hands. I heard her neck snap. He made me drag her body from the trunk to the dumpster. He would have killed me if I didn’t do as he said.”

“You had Craig killed, didn’t you? …And you hired Tuttle (that’s his name) to kill your wife? You worthless piece of crap!” Briar spat through clenched teeth. She didn’t notice that her shaking hands were still now, her voice deep with resolve.

“Yes…Yes, I had Stanton murdered, but my wife forced me to it, don’t you understand? I didn’t want to do it. It was she, not me, who wanted to live in Washington and get off this Godforsaken island. She knew I couldn’t beat Stanton or Jimmy Hinoko in a fair contest, so she said I should arrange for accidents to happen to both of them. Don't you see? I had to do it.”

“So, Jimmy Hinoko was on your list too?”

“Of course…with his family connections and money, I wouldn't have stood a chance.”

“And Kalani Stanton? How does she fit into all this?”

“Money, family, position. No matter what I did to get rid of Jimmy and Craig, I would need money and prestige to be a senator. Kalani could have given me all that. She is such a lush, though, that I could never keep her out of the bottle long enough to develop a relationship much beyond a quickie in my car, or late night bootie calls at her house.”

“So, you were planning to kill your way to the top of Hawaii's privileged class…was that the deal?”

“What do you know about Hawaii? You don't live here. I've never seen you before. Who are you, anyway?” Hilo demanded. “Oh, okay—now I recognize you; you’re the whore in the pictures. Ha-ha, Stanton and I had more in common than I thought; we were both screwing whores…"

Briar's hand was rock steady and her eyes flamed at the insults from this *waste of human skin.* All of the wickedness, dysfunction, and rejection in her life welled up in her breast. The years of pretention and posturing just to please others…all the while, starving to belong…really, just to belong somewhere. When all was said and done, she knew she only had herself…and she wasn't going to ever be humiliated or laughed at again. She was done thinking of herself as the accidental product of Donna the crack-head and Lester the scumbag. Or, as Briar…the little troublemaker from the orphanage.

"Yeah, that's right. I'm the *wahine* whore, who was supposed to take the fall for Craig's death. I'm the dumb broad that you were going to leave hanging out for his murder. Now look at us. What are we to do now, Mr. Hilo…?"

Briar was less than three feet away from Hilo when she pulled the trigger. His head ballooned in size from the supersonic impact, and he fell dead.

Briar untied Wesley's hands and his one good foot, and then helped him over to the bed. She talked to him soothingly as she inspected his injuries. She slid a pillowcase off a feather pillow to mop his bloody chest.

"My God, Wesley, what did he do to you?"

Briar stood, startled, hand covering her mouth, as she realized that the outline of a gecko had been carved into his chest. It was more of a trench line, cut and scratched into the skin—with some sort of red dye poured into the open wound.

"It's fucking food coloring…food dye," she said out loud, as she bent over and picked up a small brown bottle and held it to the light.

"We are so glad that you could make it to our party, sweetmeat. You almost missed all the fun."

Briar whirled around, stumbling backwards. Her mind couldn't comprehend exactly what was staring back at her from the doorway. She stood frozen in place as warmth ran down her legs. A totally nude Tuttle, his hairless body gleaming with oil. He was massive…his weightlifter body all pumped up and engorged. A bright neon green gecko tattoo undulated, as he simultaneously flexed and relaxed his muscles, making it appear to be crawling across his glistening chest. Blood flowed from an open wound, where his male genitals should have been. Nothing in all of Briar's experiences had prepared her for what was before her. This was death, and it had come for her. She wanted to run, jump out the window, anything to escape from what she knew was coming. She waited, terrified.

Tuttle smacked his mouth grotesquely and ran his tongue sensually across his lips, licking at the blood smeared ear to ear. His eyes were black circles of eyeliner and mascara, with lavender glitter eye shadow covering his lids. Light from the wall sconces reflected off his nicked and bleeding shaved head. Large bangle earrings hung from his ridiculous jug ears as he pirouetted across the room.

It was a horrifying sight to behold. The gecko tattoo started at his tailbone, continuing up his back and over his right shoulder, angling downward. The lizard's head stopped just above his pelvic bone, and a long red tongue disappeared into smeared blood. Tuttle was completely devoid of male genitalia. Everything was gone…penis, scrotum—the crazy bastard had neutered himself in a final desperate attempt to morph into his mother.

A nervous laugh escaped Briar's lips as Tuttle struck a pose and said in a shrill woman's voice… "I am complete now—I shan't be stopped. Dee no longer has her hold on me. I am free to do as I wish…no stopping me now." Tuttle seemed lost in his soliloquy of freedom. His eyes were unfocused; only the whites were showing. Each word was slurred and garbled as he continued incoherently.

Briar saw her chance and moved toward Wesley. She only had seconds for them to get away…

"Dee!! You can't be here…I ate you; you're dead," Tuttle bellowed, focusing on Briar. "Dee's a bad girl; she needs a good beating…yes, she does," Tuttle said, exaggerating each word.

Briar froze, her face drained of blood. It was her time; this is how it was all going to end.

Suddenly, Tuttle roared like a wild beast, and pounced—snapping Briar out of her stunned trance. She dodged to her right as she raised the pistol, firing it into Tuttle's body. He jerked from the impact, then turned on her, grabbing the pistol and throwing it across the room. Briar lashed out with a kick to his junkless crotch—missing it entirely, but soaking her foot in blood. She jabbed her outstretched fingers into his face, aiming again for the eyes.

Suddenly, Tuttle let go of her and stood up…arching his back and howling in pain. Briar scooted away. Wesley had retrieved the pistol and shot Tuttle a second time.

"Run, Briar, run. Get out of here," Wesley croaked.

Tuttle turned and ripped the pistol from Wesley's hand, pointing it at him. The handgun bucked as flame shot out of the muzzle. The round zinged by Wesley's head, burying itself in the padded headboard. Wesley rolled off the bed and started crawling toward the door. Briar grabbed a heavy baroque lamp off the dressing table and crashed it down on Tuttle's head. He shook off the impact and grabbed Briar around the waist, pulling her down, while looping the electrical cord from the lamp around her neck. Her fingers dug at the cord as he twisted it tighter, cutting into her flesh. She couldn't breathe. The light at the corners of her eyes was getting dim. She was tired, oh so tired…she just wanted to sleep…

Just then, Tuttle's body shuddered violently—his fingers releasing the tension of the cord around her neck. Air rushed back into her lungs. She gasped and sucked precious oxygen back into her lungs. She watched in slow motion as Tuttle turned toward someone calling his name. She saw Kimo standing in the doorway with a Glock 17 in his hand. A fountain of blood sprayed out of the gecko tattoo on Tuttle's back; a second fountain erupted…then a third…and a fourth. She heard a high pierced keening as Tuttle stumbled back, tripping over her. Briar successfully rolled out of the way before Tuttle landed with a thud, gasping and holding his chest.

Kimo rushed to her side, keeping his gun trained on Tuttle. He backed up, pulling her several feet away and out of Tuttle's reach. Relief flooded Briar; she rose up on an elbow and hugged Kimo tightly. Why had she ever thought she could handle this monster on her own? She watched through tear-filled eyes as Tuttle rolled onto his side, and then got up on all fours. Blood bubbled out of his nose and mouth as he swayed, mortally wounded.

"Kimo, watch it," Briar managed to squeak out.

Kimo pushed her away, rolled up, placed the pistol barrel on Tuttle's temple, and fired. Brain matter splattered everywhere.

Tuttle was finally dead—now both dickless AND headless. Briar relished the irony.

"Mo bettah I make sure," Kimo said to no one in particular. Holding his Glock to Tuttle's chest, Kimo squeezed off one last round.

The carnage of the scene burned itself indelibly into Briar's mind, just before she faded into oblivion.

Chapter 27

It had been three weeks since Jeremy Tuttle was shot and killed by Detective Kimo Kanoa. The story about the shooting of a crazed serial killer sought by the Honolulu PD was still hot gossip around the Islands…to the point that "Gecko Man" had become an ohana bugaboo, used to scare or admonish disobedient children.

During the three days immediately after the shooting, all the major news agencies and cable channels from the mainland descended on Oahu to cover the story. Political pundits couldn't get enough of how Mayor Hilo had hired a serial killer to murder Senator Stanton, and how he'd also arranged to have Gecko Man kill his wife. It was further discovered that Mayor Hilo had an open contract out to murder Jimmy Hinoko, Stanton's political rival for the senate seat race.

Jeremy Tuttle's life was turned upside down and inside out and reported on extensively. It was even rumored that Quentin Tarantino had snapped up the movie rights to Tuttle's life and was casting John Travolta to play the part. It was also being reported that Clint Eastwood bought the rights to the Mayor Hilo story, and was planning a *Dirty Harry* slant to a screenplay, neither of which held much credence.

The facts were that ten known murders had been directly attributed to Jeremy Tuttle, sixteen unsolved cases were marked as highly probable, and another dozen cold cases were being reopened. There were as many psychological theories regarding what made Tuttle the way he was as there were those who believed he was just a creation of the times. Perhaps he'd been exposed to too much violence on television and in video games growing up? The mind of this madman would be studied for decades by academia, and in the end, no one would ever really know what made Tuttle do what he did.

The one known fact, however (that most agree with), is that there are others like Tuttle out there…evolving, nurturing, feeding their inner beasts—just waiting to morph into killing machines.

Very little was reported or written about Jeremy Tuttle's other extracurricular activities, when not killing for Mayor Hilo. Nothing was written about Porter Sturgis being savagely brutalized by Tuttle, still in a coma from the massive internal damage he'd endured. Nor was much reported about the attempted murders of mainlanders Briar Malone and Wesley Barrett. The gruesome murder of Mayor Hilo's wife, who was intensely disliked by the local society, was barely a blip locally or internationally.

Briar stood on the lanai of the penthouse, morning coffee in hand, staring off to her left, at the beauty of Diamondhead's famous profile. The ocean view straight ahead was breathtaking, and as she leaned over the railing, to her right was the amazing stretch of Waikiki Beach. Sun worshipers and surfers already covered the sands as far as the eye could see. She adored everything about

Hawaii—most especially the local people that made it the paradise it was.

She turned around and walked back into the apartment; careful not to get in the way of the workmen she'd hired to repair the unbelievable amount of damage done to the unit by the killer. There were updates that the apartment needed anyway, so Auntie Cyd had opted for an entire renovation. Briar headed for the kitchen to reheat her coffee when her cell phone began chirping loudly, demanding her attention.

The caller I.D. said Wesley, so she answered, "Hi, Angel."

"Hey, Briar," Wesley sounded out of breath.

"Who's chasing you now? Oops—I don't even want to know."

"Not even remotely amusing, Bri," Wesley admonished. "Just back from a morning run on the North Shore. I left my cell in the car, and I didn't want to miss you before you left."

“I was going to call you before I boarded. Kimo should be here in a few hours to pick me up. He wanted to see how the renovations are going. The last he was here, it was…well, you know.”

“Yeah, I know.” Silence lasted a few moments as they reflected on the horrors they’d experienced. They were both fortunate to be alive.

“Tell me, how is the condo progressing?”

“Well, you won’t recognize the place; we literally gutted it. All the personal stuff is boxed and in storage until you get back and decide to set up house again. The master bedroom was stripped down to the concrete and is almost complete. No blood or brain fragments anywhere (nervous laugh). Porter’s room is finished. The bathroom is all new…”

“What about my room?” Wesley knew Briar did a makeover of his room too (since the workers were there anyway).

“I think you’ll really like the Kansas City Royals blue wall paper with the little players running around the bases…”

“You’d best be busting my balls, because if you’re serious, your little ass had better be gone by the time I get back to rip it off the walls,” he quipped.

“Don’t get your diapers in a bunch, little cousin. Your room is very tropical and serene. Trust me…you’ll love it! When have you not loved anything ever I’ve done?”

“Well, we all have our own taste,” he shot back. “And don’t get me started on some of the things you’ve done that I haven’t exactly ‘loved.’ So, Auntie Cyd says she’s staying in Hawaii with her friend Kathy until the renovations are complete? She and I have plans to meet for dinner later tonight…but tell me what she said when she first saw the place.”

“She said that you are a little chicken-shit for not having the courage to take your medicine face-to-face, rather than through me," Briar said, recalling Aunt Cyd's initial reaction to seeing the devastation done to her island home. "However, once she heard the facts surrounding the destruction, she melted with relief that both of her babies are safe."

"Did you tell her how I was almost killed by that freak, and in another couple of minutes I'd have been dead if you hadn't shown up?"

"She read the police report in full, along with hearing my side of the story. She was satisfied that we both did the right thing, and she is proud of us."

"Briar, I'll make it up to her…she knows that. We are so lucky to have her in our lives."

"And we'll both forever owe her."

"So, when will I see you again?"

"I'm not sure. I'm getting excited about the new job, but New York again…not so much. Rothschild's is a well-known and respected auction house, second only to Sotheby's in London. They have offices around the world, so no telling where I'll be assigned. My understanding is that I'll be responsible for loss investigation and recovery. It's a lucky break for me, after my fiasco at the FBI Academy."

"Well, it was their loss, Briar. That asshole agent should have kept his hands out of where they didn't belong. I still think you should sue."

"Yeah, right, Wesley…'Extra, Extra, Read all about It! Briar Malone Sues FBI!'" She mimicked her best impression of an old time newsboy.

"You're hilarious!" Wesley said. "Okay, I need to get back inside and tend to Porter, so Sharkey can leave. I love you! Call me when you get settled, send gifts—ta-ta for now." And, poof, he was gone.

Briar laughed at her cousin's silly sign off.

She wandered around the rooms, watching the painters and tile men go about changing out the place. A feeling of loneliness at having to leave brought tears to her eyes. She tried to brush off the feeling, but it suddenly enveloped her, and she started to sob. Where was her home? Where did she really belong? What was her future? Was it here in Hawaii, New York, L.A, back in the Midwest—where would she end up?

The chirp of her cell pulled her back from the brink.

"Hello."

"Dis Kimo. Is today you leave, or tomorrow?"

"It's today, Kimo. Cripes, did you forget?" she said, sounding exasperated.

"E kala mai - I wrote down wrong date. Shoots, can't make it Briar; okay I send patrol car?"

"Guess I forgot we're always on Island time here," Briar said sarcastically. "Listen, Kimo, never mind—I can get myself to the airport. Don't worry…be happy."

"Are you mad, *sistah*?"

"No way, *bruddah.* How could I ever be mad at the man who saved my life?"

"Aloha, Briar Malone."

"Aloha, Kimo, and *mahalo*."

An hour later, Briar zipped into a space in the short-term parking lot at HNL. She let the engine run for a minute for that last vibration thrill, then cut the motor. She shoved the keys under the driver's seat and placed Wesley's pistol beneath the passenger's seat. She sent a text to Auntie Cyd with the stall number, and climbed out…exposing some serious thigh in the process.

She rolled her luggage through the terminal, ignoring the whistles and stares. She was back in her element, back in control. Excitement and new adventures surely lay ahead. And, what else…what would be next on the horizon for Briar Bush Malone???

The End

Made in the USA
Charleston, SC
25 July 2015